PENGUIN BOOKS
LADAKH ADVENTURE

Deepak Dalal gave up a career in chemical engineering to write stories for children. He lives in Pune with his wife, two daughters and several dogs and cats. He enjoys wildlife, nature and the outdoors. His books include the Vikram–Aditya adventure series (for older readers) and the Feather Tales series (for younger readers). All his stories have a strong conservation theme.

A
VIKRAM–ADITYA
STORY

L A D A K H
ADVENTURE

DEEPAK
DALAL

PENGUIN BOOKS
An imprint of Penguin Random House

PENGUIN BOOKS

USA | Canada | UK | Ireland | Australia
New Zealand | India | South Africa | China

Penguin Books is part of the Penguin Random House group of companies
whose addresses can be found at global.penguinrandomhouse.com

Published by Penguin Random House India Pvt. Ltd
7th Floor, Infinity Tower C, DLF Cyber City,
Gurgaon 122 002, Haryana, India

First published by Tarini Publishing 2000
Ladakh Adventure was published by Silverfish, an imprint of Grey Oak Publishers,
in association with Westland Publications Private Limited 2013
This edition published in Penguin Books by Penguin Random House India 2020

ISBN 9780143449386

Typeset in Adobe Caslon Pro by Manipal Technologies Limited, Manipal
Printed at Thomson Press India Ltd, New Delhi

www.penguin.co.in

For Meme Chacko and David Sonam

LEARNING TO FLY

The display of Vikram's watch lit up. It was 4 a.m. The decision to rise early had been made in bed the previous evening, when he was warm, cosy and rested. But now, in the bitter cold of a Himalayan morning, his dopey, sleep-befuddled brain urged him to abandon the idea. Did he really have to watch birds at this unearthly hour? Couldn't he wait till the sun rose and the temperature climbed higher?

In moments like these, his drowsy mind could conjure several hundred reasons to slip back into divine, blissful sleep, but Vikram knew that if he did so, he would lose out on a fascinating birdwatching opportunity. Exerting all his willpower, he forced himself from the embracing warmth of his sleeping bag. Shivering, he reached for his water bottle and squirted a mouthful down his throat. Vikram realized his mistake the moment the water splashed against his tongue, but by then it was too late. The freezing liquid stung his mouth, and he gagged as he swallowed. The bottle rattled when Vikram shook it. The morning chill had half-frozen its contents.

It is impossible to move silently within the cramped confines of a tent. Its tightly zipped fabric traps sound, amplifying even the slightest movement. Vikram's school friend, Aditya, stirred and grunted. Vikram heard snatches of grumbling as he dressed. '. . . disturbing people in the middle of the night . . . selfish . . . no consideration for others . . .' Aditya's complaints flowed like a babbling Himalayan stream, forcing Vikram to hurry.

There was a sudden 'whoosh' as Vikram emerged from his tent, and he almost dropped his torch in fright. 'Noisy creatures!' he breathed, gathering his wits.

It was the birds.

Their tent was pitched beside a lake, and birds were resting on its waters. The bright beam of his torch had disturbed them, and several hundred pairs of wings had flapped in alarm. Though shaken by their sudden fluttering, Vikram still marvelled at their ability to withstand the cold. Judging from the half-frozen contents of his water bottle, ice must have formed on the lake too. Yet the birds seemed unaffected.

It was August, the warmest time of the year in Ladakh. If this was 'peak summer', wondered Vikram, then what could winter possibly be like? He shuddered at the prospect.

Aditya was still asleep when Vikram left the camp. He had scoffed at Vikram when he had invited him to come along. 'You want me to wake up at four in the morning?' Aditya had stared incredulously. 'Lose my precious sleep for a pair of birds? No way, man! You go and freeze if you want to. I've got other plans. Plans for when it is warmer—after the sun has risen. I'm going riding, at a sensible hour.'

Struggling to keep out the cold, Vikram dug his gloved hands into his pockets as he stumbled along the dark lakefront. A small pack strapped to his back contained a camera, a radio handset, a pair of binoculars, his water bottle and biscuits. A glimmer in the eastern sky forced Vikram to hurry. There was a hide some distance ahead. He had to get to it before visibility increased because the birds he intended to observe—black-necked cranes—were shy creatures. If they saw him enter the hide, they would move away and not venture anywhere near it for the rest of the day.

The hide, which was a tiny green tent, was located on the banks of the lake, about a fifteen-minute walk from the camp. Thankfully, it was still dark when Vikram arrived breathlessly by its side. There was a stool inside, which he could sit on. Observation holes had been cut at eye level on all four sides of the tent. Placing his pack on the ground, Vikram zipped the tent shut and squatted on the stool. It wasn't long before the warmth generated by his brisk walk dissipated. He buried his hands in his armpits and stamped his feet to keep out the cold.

As the colours of dawn spread across the sky, Vikram's surroundings gradually took shape. He was on the Changthang* plateau of Ladakh, 200 kilometres east of the capital, Leh. This was the northern edge of India, and the international border with China was just a few hours' drive by jeep.

---

* Tibetan word meaning 'northern plain'

The light strengthened, revealing the rolling grasslands of the Tso Kar basin. *Tso Kar* in Ladakhi means 'white lake'. Brushstrokes of white amidst the grass marked the lake. The waters of the lake were not fit for drinking. Although the area was named after the white lake, there was another river in the basin. The fresh waters of the second lake lapped just a short distance from the hide in which Vikram crouched. This lake, the water of which was good to drink, was called Tsa Tsa Phuk Tso.

During his brief stay in Ladakh, Vikram had discovered that the scale of everything in this frozen outpost of India was large, and the lakes, stretching for miles on end, were no exception. But as expressive as the adjective 'large' is, it isn't adequate to describe the grassy plain surrounding the lakes. The plain was a vast, seemingly boundless area of land. To top it all, the wonderful panorama was adorned by magnificent snow-capped mountains surrounding the Tso Kar basin.

Vikram spotted the cranes just as the rising sun tinged the snowy peaks a golden orange. There were three of them. The smallest, a baby, swam in front, while the two larger birds chaperoned behind, one on either side. According to Meme Chacko, their guardian, the little bird had been born three months ago. For a baby, the little one was fairly large. But then cranes as a species are large birds, and the two parents were huge, undoubtedly the biggest birds Vikram had seen in Ladakh.

Lifting their wings, the birds clambered on to the shore. The cranes thrilled Vikram. The bitter cold of the morning receded to a memory as he gazed at the scene before him. What majestic birds! The adult cranes were tall and elegant, the red stripe on their crowns enhancing their considerable appeal. Although their colouring was grey, it was their long, black neck that was their most distinctive feature. The fledgling, in contrast, looked plain and clumsy. It possessed neither the red stripe nor the showy black feathers on its parents' necks.

The birds were oblivious of Vikram's presence. After a quick scan, swaying their heads from side to side, they settled down to the important task of feeding. The adult birds pecked at the ground, plucking at roots and skimming their beaks above the grass, seeking insects. The baby bird, however, wasn't interested in feeding. It had other plans. The young bird spread its wings, thrusting them wide. It then lowered and spread them again.

Vikram watched in fascination. Was the baby learning to fly? Yes, indeed, it seemed so. The bird ran forward, flapping its wings. Vikram laughed. So awkward were the bird's movements that they seemed comical. The juvenile creature tangled its wings with its feet and almost tumbled to the ground. Its frantic manoeuvres were clumsy—so unlike the fluid, easy movements of its parents.

Vikram was aware that the spectacle he beheld was a rare one. In India, black-necked cranes are found only in Ladakh. Just fifteen pairs nest in the far-flung corners of the Changthang plateau. Local people treasure the birds, never harming them. Vikram's host for his Ladakh holiday, Meme Chacko, had fallen in love with the cranes when he had first come across them while serving as a soldier in Ladakh.

After retiring from the army, Meme Chacko had studied the available literature on black-necked cranes and discovered that little is known about them. In fact, of the fifteen species of cranes that exist on our planet, black-necked cranes were the last to be discovered. Their habits, their numbers, their migration patterns were all a mystery, never having been subjected to scientific investigation. Meme Chacko had decided to take it upon himself to study the birds and had returned to the lonely plateau. For the past seven years, he had not missed a single summer in Ladakh, driving up from his native town Bangalore, arriving before the cranes, waiting to greet them on their return from their wintering grounds.

Meme Chacko was a thin, upright, grey-haired gentleman. Looking at him, no one would guess he was seventy years old. Not only was Meme Chacko lean and fit but also the things he did often put younger men to shame. He thought nothing of wading through semi-frozen lakes to get close to the birds, or travelling for days across inhospitable terrain or camping out alone for months on end in the chilly high altitudes of Ladakh. The title *meme* means 'grandfather' in Ladakhi, and it had been fondly prefixed to his name by the local nomads of Changthang, who, over the years, had grown to know and admire the sprightly old soldier.

Meme Chacko was also a great friend of Vikram's father, and when he had learnt that the boys were planning to visit Ladakh, he had promised to take them on one of his safaris to the Changthang plateau. If Meme Chacko had not had to travel the previous evening, he would have been standing right beside Vikram, in the hide.

Vikram recalled the incident that had led to Meme Chacko's abrupt departure. Just the previous day, as the sun had set, a messenger on horseback had come to their camp with news that a pair of cranes had been spotted at Staglung. Vikram had seen the gleam of excitement in Meme Chacko's eyes. When it came to cranes, there was no holding the old soldier back. Staglung wasn't far, and he could get there in a few hours in his jeep. Apologizing to the boys, he had left almost immediately.

'Everything is set up for you two,' he had told them before leaving. 'There are provisions for three to four days, and Nanju, the cook, will stay behind. I am leaving little Tsering at the camp with you. I must go now. Wish me luck,' he had smiled, and had driven off in his jeep, promising to return soon.

The hatchling was leaping in the air, flapping its wings. It was working hard, pouring energy into its endeavour. With sharp, high-pitched calls, the little bird concentrated on its task.

Was it really so difficult to fly, wondered Vikram? The bird's efforts appeared to be bearing little fruit. There were energetic leaps followed by vigorous flapping and loud calling as it sank back to the ground. Then another leap, more flapping and more cries of frustration.

Vikram saw an orange glow on the little crane's wings. The feathers of the larger birds shone too. The sun had cleared the ring of mountains, and its light now bathed the Tso Kar plain. 'About time,' Vikram muttered under his breath. He had borne the cold long enough.

A lone horseman was crossing the plain in the distance. Vikram shifted his attention from the birds, focusing his binoculars on the rider.

Aditya!

Yes, it was Aditya astride a small brown horse. So he had woken up! Vikram was impressed. He had doubted his friend's commitment to his morning plan on hearing his drowsy grunts in the tent. As Vikram watched, the horse began to trot. Vikram could clearly see Aditya's face through the binoculars. He was urging his mount to move faster. Vikram smiled when he saw the glee on Aditya's face as his steed broke into a canter and then into an unrestrained gallop. On the massive Tso Kar plain, the horse was no more than a dot, like a beetle scurrying through the grass. There was something wild and primitive about the sight. The scene could well have been from another age. A horse running free, the wide grassy plain, the mountains and the pale blue sky above.

Far to Vikram's left, where the rim of the basin rose towards the snow-capped peaks, a group of horses was grazing beside a white tent. The tent belonged to the Changpas* who lived on the Tso Kar plain, and it was one of their horses that Aditya had borrowed.

---

* Nomadic herders of the Changthang plateau

Vikram could see his own camp too. Three brightly coloured tents nestled in the grass on the banks of the freshwater lake. Nanju, the cook, and little Tsering were crouched beside a kerosene stove. The binoculars brought them into sharp focus. They were both clutching steaming mugs. Despite the distance, Vikram could see the deep red colour on young Tsering's cheeks. Meme Chacko had said Tsering was nine years old. Though he did not speak a word of English or Hindi, both Vikram and Aditya had taken a liking to the little boy who always had a ready smile for them.

As Vikram lowered his binoculars, he detected movement on the water. On its calm, glass-like surface, he saw a ripple. He trained his binoculars on it. A black object, triangular in shape, was nearing the shore. Vikram spotted a pair of eyes, ears and a black snout. Was it a dog? There were yellow dots above the eyes. Changpa dogs were black and most had prominent yellow spots above their eyes. The black, hairy animals were strong and helped their nomad masters herd their sheep and goats. Though gentle with children, they stood their ground against wolves, often foiling their attempts to take sheep in the high pastures.

But on this occasion, the sight of the dog brought a chill to Vikram. The animal was swimming towards the birds. Meme Chacko had said that dogs were a menace to the cranes. Adult birds evaded them by flying away, but chicks, especially those that couldn't fly, were easy prey. He had said that the Changpa dogs endangered

11

the very survival of the cranes. 'There are just fifteen nesting pairs of these birds in India,' he had told them. 'Each pair gives birth to only one chick every year. The numbers are so low that every individual matters. The loss of even a single chick has a bearing on the future of the species. These dogs—' Meme Chacko had clenched his jaw, 'Don't mistake me; I love dogs, but I detest these animals. They raid crane nests, steal their eggs, and if the chick is born, they kill the helpless little creature. I do not like to shoot animals, but sometimes I am forced to kill these dogs.'

Vikram had no gun; all he possessed was a camera and a pair of binoculars. There was nothing he could do to protect the birds. Maybe he could alert them . . . but events unfolded quicker than Vikram's thoughts. The attack took place so fast that he barely had time to blink.

The dog flashed forward the moment it reached the shore. All three birds were taken by surprise. The parents flapped their wings in alarm, rising into the air. But it wasn't the adult birds the dog was after; it shot forward with startling speed towards the baby crane.

Vikram was helpless; there was little he could do except watch. The hatchling shrieked. Tilting its head, the little bird ran. The dog pursued. The bird flailed its wings desperately. The distance between the hunter and prey shrank. The bird called loudly, wailing for its parents. The big birds flew behind the dog, screeching at the animal. Elsewhere, geese honked and ducks swam away to the far shore of the lake.

The chick was doomed. It simply could not outrun the dog. Vikram wished he had a gun. At this moment, even he would have shot the dog.

The dog was right beside the little bird, just a couple of metres separating them. The chick leapt, springing as high as it could. Its wings spread outwards, probably for one final time, thought Vikram. They beat downward, pressing against the still morning air. In the twinkling of an eye, the wings spread once more and then beat down again.

Vikram couldn't believe his eyes. The hatchling was flying. It lifted skywards as the dog yelped and rose on his hind legs. The adult birds flew forward encouraging their young one. But all was not well with the little bird. Despite frantically beating its wings, it lost height, sinking to the ground. The dog barked triumphantly and leapt forward. The baby crane ran, stretching its wings. For a while it did not beat them, it just kept running, then it leapt and flapped its wings. The bird soared skywards.

Vikram watched in fascination. There was no more frantic flapping. Now the wingbeats were controlled, rhythmic and relaxed. The dog had come to a halt once again. Vikram heard a high-pitched whine followed by a yelping bark. Some distance ahead, the little crane sat on the ground again. But the dog made no effort to resume the chase. The adult birds spread their wings and circled above their offspring. The young bird ran again with its wings outstretched. It took off effortlessly, rising into the sky. The three birds made a pretty picture as they flew away towards the white waters of Tso Kar.

YAK RESCUE

There was no point staying on in the hide. Vikram stepped out and started on the long trek back to camp. The sun was warm on his back, and there was a rumbling in his stomach. It was time for a hot, wholesome meal. Nanju made excellent aloo parathas and had promised to prepare them for breakfast.

A strange sound, outlandish in the rarefied atmosphere of Tso Kar, disturbed Vikram's musings. It seemed to originate from the campsite. Looking up, Vikram spotted the source.

A jeep.

Had Meme Chacko returned? No. The vehicle wasn't his. It was a large four-door jeep, not the compact Gypsy that Meme Chacko owned. Who could it be, wondered Vikram? And why was the vehicle being driven so fast?

The jeep was roaring away from the camp and something or somebody was running after it. Vikram halted, puzzled. Was it Nanju, the cook? Vikram raised his binoculars. It was Nanju. His hand was raised, and he was waving a fist at the departing vehicle as he ran. Something had gone wrong at the camp. Vikram broke into a run. Five minutes of accelerated sprinting brought him to the tents.

Nanju rushed forward to meet him. His brown face had turned ashen. 'The boy!' he shouted in Hindi. 'They have taken our little Tsering!'

Vikram stared at the cook uncomprehendingly. Nanju seized Vikram's hand and swung him round till he faced the departing vehicle.

'Those people in the jeep! They have taken Tsering. They came here asking for tea. I went to the kitchen tent and they grabbed Tsering and dragged him to their jeep. I heard Tsering's cry, but by the time I came out, they were driving away. They have taken him!'

Tsering!

Vikram stared after the jeep. Why would anyone want to take Tsering away? What had the boy done to deserve this? Vikram clenched his fists. There was little he could do. He had no vehicle in which to follow the jeep. He was helpless . . . or was he?

Aditya!

Aditya had ridden towards the Polokong La pass. The jeep was headed in the same direction. Shielding his eyes from the sun, Vikram gazed at the pass. At the head of the pass, almost at its very top, he spotted a shadow. His binoculars transformed the shadow into a familiar figure. Aditya.

Vikram's mind raced. Both he and Aditya had handsets—two pocket-sized radios that functioned within a range of ten kilometres. Meme Chacko had thoughtfully left them behind for the boys to use. Vikram could contact Aditya and ask him to get Tsering back. He reached into his pack and retrieved his set. Extending the aerial, he pressed the 'talk' button.

The morning's exhilaration was something Aditya would remember for a long time. Cold wind had streamed past his face as his Ladakhi mount had run wild across the grasslands. It was difficult to describe the emotion—possibly a feeling of uninhibited freedom, or maybe it was just the sheer joy of the moment. Whatever it was, that feeling had gone to his head. He had whooped and had urged his willing steed to greater speeds. The feisty little creature had responded wonderfully, pounding across the grass, enjoying the run as much as Aditya.

When they reached the incline leading to the pass, the horse eased its stride. A stream flowed beside their track, and somewhere close to the crest of the pass, the horse halted to drink. Aditya dismounted. Extracting a cup from his backpack, he scooped water for himself. When he was done, he leaned forward and washed his face.

Aditya was a tall boy, standing a little over six feet. His long, straggly hair tumbled forward as he knelt beside the stream. He splashed water on his face and scrubbed away spiritedly. But the near-freezing temperature of the mountain stream defeated him. Despite his best efforts, he was forced to give up when his fingers lost feeling and a stinging sensation numbed his cheeks. It was while he was shaking his fingers that his handset beeped.

Vikram!

What did Vikram want, wondered Aditya as he pulled the radio from his pack and pressed the push-to-talk (PTT) button.

'Morning, Vikram,' he said breezily.

'Aditya, listen to me!'

Aditya tensed, sensing the urgency in Vikram's voice.

'Look back towards Tsa Tsa Phuk Tso. Can you see a jeep? Over.'

'Yes, I can,' replied Aditya, wondering what was bothering Vikram.

'Tsering is in that jeep. He has been abducted! Over.'

'What?!' exclaimed Aditya. He could see the jeep. It had crossed the lake and was heading in his direction.

'Yes, he has been kidnapped. I don't know why and neither does Nanju. The jeep is headed for the pass. Do something Aditya, get Tsering back!'

'What can I—' Aditya paused. Then pressing the PTT button, he continued. 'I'll speak to Dorje, he might help. We'll see what we can do. Don't worry, we'll try something. I'd better go. There isn't much time. Bye.'

Vikram's voice came through once again. 'Best of luck,' he wished.

Aditya grabbed the reins of his horse. Polokong La pass was barely a kilometre ahead. Aditya urged his steed into a canter. The path was steep and though the horse flagged, Aditya willed it forward.

Dorje's camp was at the pass. Dorje was a Changpa, a nomadic herder, who herded sheep, goats and yaks.

Vikram and Aditya had met Dorje and his people through Meme Chacko. Meme Chacko was popular amongst all the Changpas of the region, and any friends of the retired soldier were accepted as friends of the Changpas. The horse Aditya was riding had been lent by Dorje.

The Changpas live mostly in tents. In Ladakhi, their tents are called *reebos*, and the Changpas are often referred to as the reebo people. Aditya spotted sheep and goats as he neared the top of the pass. There were tents pitched beyond the pass and yaks were grazing beside them. An idea came to Aditya when he saw the yaks. Yes, if they acted quickly, it would be possible to halt the jeep.

Aditya forced his tiring mount towards a black reebo. Dorje stood beside it. Despite the frigid morning cold, Dorje was attired in just a T-shirt and trousers. His tanned and weathered face indicated the outdoor life he led.

'You have come,' he greeted, speaking in Hindi.

Aditya smiled at the Changpa.

The entrance to the reebo was pulled back, and a middle-aged lady stuck her head out.

'*Jule*,'* said Aditya, folding his hands.

'Jule, jule,' greeted Padma, Dorje's wife. Padma wore traditional flowy Ladakhi robes. Like Dorje, her face was heavily tanned.

Aditya smiled at Padma. Then he turned to Dorje, and clasping the Changpa's shoulder, he led him to a dusty knoll from where they could look down on the Tso Kar plain.

---

* A greeting in Ladakhi

Aditya pointed to the jeep, which was now labouring up the incline leading to the pass.

'That jeep,' he told Dorje in Hindi. 'We have to stop it. It must be halted here.'

'Okay,' said Dorje, not really understanding what Aditya was saying. Sensing the Changpa's confusion, Aditya quickly explained the situation to him.

'They have stolen your little boy, Tsering?' questioned Dorje after listening to Aditya.

Aditya nodded.

'Why?'

Aditya replied truthfully. 'I have no idea. Really, I do not know. But that doesn't matter. We have to get him back.' Aditya was looking at the pass as he spoke. The jeep was slowly climbing up a mud track littered with boulders. The track was in bad shape; in many places, all traces of it had been washed away. Given the road's condition, the jeep would not be able to move fast. Aditya estimated he had five minutes before the vehicle reached the reebos. The road had to be blocked by then.

Speaking quickly to Dorje, Aditya spelt out his plan. The Changpa listened quietly, nodding occasionally.

'We block the road there,' said Dorje, pointing to a spot some hundred metres down the track. 'The path is steep and narrow there. It is a good place. You wait here, I will do it.'

Dorje ran to a white tent where two boys stood. He spoke to them in Ladakhi, gesticulating animatedly, pointing often at the cattle and the approaching jeep.

19

The exchange was short. The boys split up soon after, one making for the yaks, the other striding briskly in the direction of the goats and sheep.

Leading his horse by the bridle Aditya followed the boy walking to the yaks. Yaks are massive animals, as big as the enormous gaurs of Mudumalai. In length, they equal two cows standing one behind the other; and in height, the animals stand tall—four feet at the shoulder. Bull-like horns thrust from their heads, and thick mats of woolly hair cover every inch of their bodies.

Aditya was surprised at how quickly the yaks responded to the boy. All it took was a few high-pitched calls and the animals started to move. The woolly beasts bunched together and plodded towards the track.

The jeep's dust plume was closer now. The path had to be blocked fast.

The yaks reached the track and walked briskly along it. Ahead was a gully with walls on either side. Dorje's instructions to the boy must have been faultless, because he was leading the animals towards this narrow section.

Pulling his horse along, Aditya ran ahead of the yaks. The gully was long, about hundred metres in length, a perfect spot for an ambush. There was no exit for the jeep if it was halted here. The rock walls on either side would prevent it from manoeuvring either left or right. A bend in the track hid the gully from any vehicle travelling uphill. In fact, the jeep was not visible from where Aditya stood. Its dust trail, however, revealed its position. Aditya swallowed; the dust cloud was drawing dangerously close.

Aditya ran, dragging his horse up the gully wall. There was no tree to tie the horse to. Hoping that the animal would not wander far, he trailed its reins on the ground. From where he stood, he could see both the jeep and the gully. The reebos were visible too. Aditya turned to the Changpa settlement, and the sight he saw drew a smile to his lips. The goats and sheep were coming. There were hundreds of them, all heading for the gully. Dorje and two others were herding them forward.

Aditya settled himself next to his horse. The jeep would certainly be forced to halt. The Changpas had done what he had asked of them. Now it was up to him.

The jeep's engine droned loudly. A whiff of diesel fouled the morning air. The yaks were milling in the gully, rubbing shoulders in its narrow confines. Aditya crouched next to his horse as the jeep rounded the bend.

There was the sudden blaring of a horn. The yaks snorted, backing away. Dorje and the boys yelled sharply at them. The yaks stayed their ground. Caught between the honking vehicle and the shouting humans, they stamped their feet and swung their heads, raking the air with their horns.

The jeep came to a halt. The honking stopped and a brown head popped out, shouting in Ladakhi. Dorje shouted back, holding his hand to his ear. The driver waved a fist. Then he thumped it against his door.

Aditya rose. Keeping low, he scampered towards the jeep. He slid down the wall into the gully. The driver had resumed shouting. On the far side, Dorje was gesticulating.

Nobody noticed Aditya. On his hands and knees, he covered the distance to the vehicle. Crouching, he rested his palms gently on its grimy fender. He then slowly raised himself and peered through the rear window.

Tsering was in the back seat. Beside him sat a second man with a brown, tanned face. One of his hands firmly grasped Tsering's arm.

The horn blared once again as the driver pressed down on it. The sound was deafening inside the gully. But the noise was welcome, providing the perfect cover for Aditya.

Aditya crouched below the rear door. There was pandemonium in the gully. Yaks snorted, sheep called, goats bleated, dogs barked and the Changpas added to the chorus with their high-pitched calls. The horn blared incessantly.

Aditya grasped the handle and jerked the door open. His hands shot forward, grabbing Tsering's free arm. With both hands, he yanked Tsering towards him, pulling with all his strength. The surprise was absolute. Although the man holding Tsering had a firm grip on the boy, Aditya's sudden, powerful tug was sufficient to free the boy. Tsering came flying out of the door. Caught off balance, Aditya fell to the ground with Tsering sprawling over him.

Aditya was up in a flash.

The man in the back seat had not reacted yet. There was a dumbfounded expression on his face.

Aditya spotted streaks of red on Tsering's cheek. The boy had fallen face down and cut his cheek. But in spite of his pain, Tsering's delight shone through. There was a big grin on his face.

'Come on!' Aditya cried urgently.

Tsering did not require encouragement. Leaping to his feet, he dashed after Aditya who was already running down the track. Aditya scaled the wall of the gully and sped towards his horse. Thankfully, the animal hadn't wandered. Grabbing the reins, he waited for Tsering. 'Hurry!' he shouted impatiently at the boy.

Tsering's abductors had emerged from the jeep and were sprinting down the gully. Panting, Tsering reached Aditya's side. Grasping the boy, Aditya lifted him on to the horse and mounted behind him. Yelling at the animal, Aditya kicked it forward.

TIBETAN MYSTERY

Aditya let the horse run. The animal tore across the mountainside, choosing its own path. After a couple of minutes of fast running, Aditya reined in his steed. Turning, he looked back.

His pursuers had wisely refrained from trying to outrun a horse. They were still at the gully. They stood, heads bowed in discussion. Behind them, Dorje was herding his goats and sheep back to the reebos. The yaks were ambling towards the mountain slopes.

Aditya loosened the reins, allowing the horse to browse the sandy track. There was no imminent danger. The mountainside the horse had run along was sloping and treacherous, impossible for the jeep to navigate. If the men wanted to chase the boys, they would have to pursue them on foot. There was time for Aditya to collect his thoughts. His head was abuzz with questions. Who were these men? What did they want with Tsering? What would they do now?

Tsering could possibly answer most of his questions. But this brought no comfort to Aditya. Little Tsering spoke only Tibetan.

Back at the gully, the two men were still talking.

Aditya chose to wait. He would decide his course of action only after he was sure of their next move. He stared at the men, trying to guess their motives. What was it that had compelled them to seek Tsering in this remote corner of India?

Aditya's thoughts drifted back to the time they had met Tsering. Was there something they had all missed? Some clue that could throw light on his kidnapping? What was so special about Tsering?

Aditya and Vikram had first met Tsering at a village called Sumdo, a collection of ramshackle huts set in a barren, desolate valley—a most uninspiring place. Yet tucked deep within Sumdo's stony bosom, the boys had stumbled upon an unlikely surprise: a school. Not an ordinary government school but a wonderful, heart-warming school with brightly painted buildings, meticulously maintained grounds and a crowd of happy, smiling children with red cheeks. It was a boarding school for Tibetan children, and Tsering was studying there. The headmaster of the school was a friend of Meme Chacko's and they had stopped by to meet him.

At first glance, Tsering had seemed no different from the children gathered there, with his short, cropped hair, smiling face and typical Tibetan features. But even before they made his acquaintance, Vikram and Aditya had sensed something about him that set him apart from the others. While all the others had chorused 'jule' when they'd entered, Tsering had simply smiled, flashing eyes that resembled deep pools of light.

It was in the headmaster's office that Meme Chacko had casually mentioned that Tsering would be joining them on their excursion to Tso Kar. Vikram and Aditya had naturally been curious about Tsering, but when they tried to converse with the boy as they drove away, they discovered it wasn't possible. They had pressed Meme Chacko for information, but he had not been forthcoming. He had answered their queries with grunts and had always changed the subject. All he had said was, 'Tsering is an important child who has been entrusted to my care. As far as you two are concerned, he is the cook's helper. That's what you will say to anyone asking questions about him. You are not to reveal that we picked him up from the Sumdo school. He will be with us till we return to Leh. It's my job to deliver him there safely.'

Meme Chacko had held firm and refused to answer questions. 'Nothing till we deliver him safely to Leh,' he had said. 'When he is secure and no longer in my care, I will tell you whatever I can. Save your queries for then.'

Now the mystery surrounding Tsering had deepened, and there was no Meme Chacko to turn to. Vikram and he had become unwitting bodyguards. They had to protect Tsering but they had no idea from whom or why.

The handset suddenly beeped, startling both Aditya and Tsering.

Aditya reached for his pack and then stopped. He was in full view of the kidnappers. It would be unwise to pull out the set and publicize that he was in radio contact with Vikram. There was a fold in the mountains ahead where the men would not be able to see him. Aditya started forward, guiding his mount to the fold.

The fold lay behind a hillock whose slopes bordered the Tso Kar plain. Just before the path rounded the mound, Aditya tugged at the reins, restraining his mount. Turning, he looked back.

The kidnappers had finally swung into action. One was jogging down the track in their direction. The other was in the jeep, driving back down the pass. Aditya heard Tsering mutter something in an angry voice.

'What did you say?' inquired Aditya.

Tsering spoke rapidly, pointing vigorously at the pass. Aditya nodded. 'I understand,' he said solemnly. 'I understand every word you say.'

The little Tibetan grinned.

Aditya smiled and raised his palm. 'Give me a five!' he said.

Though Tsering did not understand Aditya, he raised his hand and their palms met.

Aditya's big hand enveloped Tsering's little fist. Holding it tight, he stared into the boy's eyes. 'Don't worry, Tsering,' he promised. 'We'll find a way to beat them.'

The boy winked and Aditya winked back.

Aditya shifted his attention to the kidnappers. He had hoped that they would give up and go home. But that wasn't the case. Leave alone abandoning their pursuit, they had instead doubled their efforts by splitting up.

Aditya believed that the mountains were his best bet. The plains of Tso Kar were out of the question. The vehicle

27

would easily outpace his horse and corner him. Up here on the rocky slopes of the mountain, the jeep was not a threat, but the man running down the track most definitely was. Aditya urged his horse quickly round the hillock, and when he was out of sight of both the jeep and the jogging man, he pulled out his radio set.

'Vikram, are you there?' he began.

Vikram's voice came through loud and clear. 'Sorry for calling while you were in view of the kidnappers . . . My mistake. I wasn't thinking. I can see you right now hiding behind that hill. If you can't see me, it's because I'm sitting behind the tent.' Vikram paused. 'I suggest you and Tsering stay up in the mountains. You are safe there. That second kidnapper is following you, but he's dreaming if he believes he can keep up with a horse. Food will be a problem, but don't worry your head about it. Nanju is preparing a meal, and I'll bring it across as soon as he is done. Do you see that abandoned Changpa settlement on my side of the lake? I'll ride out in that direction. Meet me in the mountains above the settlement. Okay?'

'Sounds good, Vikram,' replied Aditya. 'Get lots of food, I'm starving. And wait a minute, master Tsering wants to talk to you.'

Aditya watched the little boy. He had not taught him how to use a radio, yet he seemed to know what to do. He pressed the PTT button.

'Vikram . . . *Dhanyawad*!' said Tsering and released the button.

'Don't thank me,' replied Vikram, speaking in Hindi. 'You are our friend.'

Aditya saw Tsering's eyes light up when the word 'friend' crackled from the speaker. He obviously understood its meaning.

Aditya took the set back from Tsering. 'Enough chattering for now, Vikram. I better get moving. Our friend the jogger is getting close. Bring the food fast and let's meet above the settlement. Over and out.'

After ten minutes of riding, when Aditya looked back, he saw the jogger resting at the hillock. A short while later, the man was walking along the track. The jogger was now a walker.

Aditya relaxed, allowing his horse to ease its stride. Down below, the jeep had come to a halt. Aditya surveyed the Tso Kar plain. Although it had been obvious all along, it struck him only now that there was not a single tree on its great expanse. There was absolutely no cover on the plain; no place to hide, or for that matter, no spot to shelter behind and plot an ambush. The lack of cover wasn't confined to the lake basin alone. It extended to the mountains. The slope on which Aditya rode was sandy and barren. Ladakh, as everyone had said, was indeed a desert.

Vikram was visible in the distance, trotting along on his horse. He was in plain sight of the jeep driver, and Aditya was sure that the man was tracking his movements. In the high-altitude landscape of Ladakh, it is possible to see for miles on end. Up there the intense clarity of vision overcomes the distortion of distances. It mattered little that Vikram and Aditya were several kilometres from the jeep driver. Their actions were like an open book to the kidnappers. Outwitting the men was going to be difficult, if not impossible. It didn't require a genius to conclude that the boys planned to meet. Their converging paths loudly advertised their intentions.

The two friends caught up with one another a little after 9 a.m. Tsering solemnly shook Vikram's hand and said 'dhanyawad' once more.

'Where's the food?' demanded Aditya, dispensing with manners.

Vikram eyed Aditya amusedly. 'You could at least say, "please",' he said.

Ignoring him, Aditya grabbed the rucksack tied to Vikram's saddle. Squatting, he attacked the meal in earnest. Tsering settled himself next to Aditya, and while the food was being consumed, Vikram trained his binoculars on the jeep below.

The vehicle was parked on the far side of Tsa Tsa Phuk Tso, some ten kilometres away, estimated Vikram. The jogger had abandoned the chase a long time ago and had descended to the Tso Kar plain. The jeep had driven across to meet him, and since then the vehicle hadn't moved. Vikram could discern two shadows inside the jeep.

'Look!' exclaimed Aditya, his mouth stuffed with a chapatti. 'I see a jeep at Polokong La pass.'

Vikram swung his binoculars around. Yes, a jeep had appeared, and it was driving slowly down the pass. For a moment, Vikram's heart leapt. Meme Chacko . . . Could it be him? But the jeep was black, not the familiar green of the vehicle they had driven up in. 'It isn't Meme Chacko,' he said. 'Somebody else, possibly tourists.'

Lowering the binoculars, Vikram sat next to Tsering, who beamed and offered him a chapatti. Vikram smiled and declined. Then placing his arm around the boy, he looked him in the eyes. 'Tsering,' he said, speaking slowly and clearly. 'Who are these men?'

Tsering gazed at Vikram. Then he pointed at the parked jeep and said, 'Tibetan.'

Aditya paused, chapatti in hand.

'Why?' asked Vikram, shrugging his shoulders in an exaggerated manner. 'Why are Tibetans following you?'

Holding Vikram's gaze, Tsering pointed to himself and said, 'Me . . . Tibet.'

Aditya frowned.

Vikram leaned forward. 'You,' he pointed at Tsering, 'Jeep . . . Tibet.'

Tsering smiled, nodding several times.

'Does that mean that these men want to take him to Tibet?' asked Aditya.

'I think so,' replied Vikram. 'It seems possible . . . The Tibetan border is only a few hours from here.'

'The plot thickens,' said Aditya.

Vikram smiled but did not say anything.

'Let's see,' said Aditya. 'We have a pair of Tibetans chasing us. They want to take away a little boy who is in our custody, and it appears that they want to take him to Tibet. Am I correct, Vikram?'

'Yes, and you can add that the little boy does not want to go with them,' said Vikram.

Aditya nodded. 'Yes, the boy has demonstrated that quite clearly to us. Also, the boy knows who these men are, but poor fellow, he can't communicate this to us. Complicating matters even further is the fact that we know nothing about the boy. Tsering himself is a mystery. When we inquired about him, we were told not to ask questions. Of course, the elderly gentleman who refused to answer our questions has since conveniently disappeared.' Aditya paused and looked at Vikram. 'Interesting situation, isn't it? Something right up your street, Vikram. You're the brainy one, what do you suggest?'

'How about learning Tibetan?' suggested Vikram. 'Tsering can give us a crash course. Then, when we have mastered the language, he can explain and solve the mystery.'

Aditya shook his head. 'I'm not good at languages. It might be easier teaching him Hindi instead.'

The boys laughed. Tsering joined in with a loud guffaw.

Aditya and Tsering resumed their meal.

A cloud stole across the sun, and Vikram shivered as the temperature dropped sharply. The kidnappers were still parked on the far side of the lake. The second jeep—the new arrival—was driving down to the Tso Kar plain. Vikram hoped its occupants were tourists. The more the people in the basin, the better it was for them. This was the first jeep; others could arrive later in the day.

When Aditya was satiated and was licking his fingers, Vikram spoke, 'I'm going to head back down in a short while.'

Aditya stared. 'Whatever for? You out of your mind? Those men will corner you with their jeep before you can blink.'

Vikram shook his head. 'Uh-uh. It's Tsering they want, not me. If I have Tsering, they'll come after me, but they won't bother if I'm alone. You stay here with Tsering, I'll head down.'

Aditya wasn't convinced. 'But why . . . why do you want to go down?'

'It's obvious they can't do anything to us while we are up here. Their jeep is useless in the mountains, and we have horses, which they don't. We are safe in the mountains, the men know that. But they also know our camp is down there. Our supplies, our tent, our shelter, our food—it's obvious we will have to return sometime or the other. We can stay away all day, but what about the night? They are waiting for the evening, Aditya. They know we will have to go back to camp. If they are going to try once more for Tsering, they will strike sometime during the night—when we are huddled inside our tents.'

'So,' said Aditya. 'We could stay here. All you have to do is bring the tents and the sleeping bags up into the mountains.'

'Shifting camp isn't easy, Aditya. They aren't stupid, they'll understand what we are up to the moment we start dismantling the tents. Carrying all that material is cumbersome. Their jeep will easily intercept us on the plain.'

'Then just bring the sleeping bags. You could slip them out from the tent without alerting anyone. Forget the tents, all we need is our bags and warm clothes. Tsering and I will be okay.'

'We could do that,' agreed Vikram, 'but I was thinking of something else. There's a possibility that we might have help at hand. That jeep, the one crossing between the lakes, it could be a tourist jeep. I want to talk to whoever is travelling in it. They could help us.'

'You think so? Come on, Vikram! They are on holiday. What are you going to tell them? Help . . . These men are trying to kidnap my Tibetan companion. Abandon your holiday, please put your plans on hold and help me!'

Vikram held up his hands. 'Will you let me finish? I'm not thinking about that at all. I'm thinking about the night. Maybe I can talk them into camping close to us. And that jeep won't be the only one. It's still morning. There's plenty of time. I'm certain more tourists will arrive later. If we all camp together we can take advantage of safety in numbers. There are only two kidnappers.'

Aditya pursed his lips. 'We could do that,' he said thoughtfully.

'And there's another thing,' continued Vikram. 'Splitting up will keep the men on their toes. They'll have to double their efforts instead of limiting their attention to one area. We can confuse them further if you disappear behind the mountains.' Vikram laughed. 'I'd love to see their reaction when Tsering is no longer visible and his whereabouts become uncertain.'

Vikram had Aditya's attention now. Although Aditya wasn't entirely convinced, he had faith in Vikram's thinking, considering how his ideas had gotten them out of sticky situations several times.

Squatting beside Aditya, Vikram discussed every possibility and contingency he could think of, carefully analyzing responses to each one. The radio handsets were crucial to their plans—a distinct advantage in their battle with the kidnappers—providing great flexibility. Vikram could respond to developments. He could change strategy at any moment and inform Aditya accordingly. Without the handsets, Vikram doubted whether he would have left Aditya's side.

RADIO CONTACT

Aditya and Tsering parted company with Vikram. While Vikram rode down to the camp, they climbed higher into the mountains.

Thin, feathery clouds had spread themselves in the sky. The weather was of the T-shirt variety, comfortable as long as the sun was out and chilly the moment its rays were blocked. At present, the sun was shining fiercely and Aditya's body was damp with sweat as he struggled up a steep incline. Aditya held the reins of his horse as it plodded behind him. It had been an exhausting morning for the animal, and he did not want to tax it any further. Tsering climbed silently beside Aditya.

Both Aditya and Tsering had to rest often as their lungs battled to extract oxygen from the thin mountain air. At lower altitudes, Aditya might have ascended the mountain without pausing, but here on the Changthang plateau of Ladakh, circumstances were different.

The Polokong La pass is 16,000 feet above sea level. There is a vast difference between oxygen availability at sea level and at 16,000 feet. At sea level, the atmosphere is dense, and oxygen is available in plenty. But at 16,000 feet, the atmosphere is considerably rarer, and the availability of the life-sustaining element decreases drastically.

Earlier, when Aditya and Vikram had arrived in Ladakh, they had both felt breathless on landing at Leh airport. Leh—the capital of Ladakh—is at 12,000 feet above sea level, and the drop in oxygen levels had immediately hit them. Meme Chacko had forced them to rest for four days in Leh so that their bodies could acclimatize to the lack of oxygen. 'We're headed for the Changthang region, which is even higher than Leh,' he had told them. 'I don't want problems up there. There are no hospitals or doctors to look after you if you fall sick. So you had better rest and acclimatize yourselves here. Don't take this lightly. Mountain sickness is dangerous. That's the sickness you get when your body can't cope with the lack of oxygen. Many die in Ladakh each year because of this condition. So be careful.'

Aditya was thoroughly acclimatized to the sparse Ladakh air, yet he suffered acute breathlessness on the climb. He understood now why mountaineers carry oxygen on the upper slopes of the Himalayas. There just isn't sufficient oxygen in the air to sustain a strenuous activity like climbing. Aditya adopted a rhythm. He would climb a few metres, pushing himself as far as he could until his lungs forced a halt. The next minute would be spent gasping for oxygen and calming his heaving chest. The process of climb, halt, climb, halt was repeated over and over again. The ascent was an exhausting experience, and Aditya dearly wished he had an oxygen cylinder strapped to his back.

There was no elation when they reached the top, only a sense of thankfulness that the climb was over. The lakes and the basin were now far below. Vikram was a tiny blip riding towards the camp. The second jeep had driven across the lakes and was parked close to their camp. The kidnappers were still at the same spot, on the far side of Tsa Tsa Phuk Tso.

After regaining his breath, Aditya dug out his binoculars from his pack and focused them on the kidnappers. Both were sitting on the bonnet of their jeep, gazing up in his direction. Aditya raised his hand and waved at them. Tsering did the same, a mischievous grin on his face. They both burst out laughing when one of the kidnappers shook a fist at them.

They did not linger long at the pass. A chilly wind forced them to hurry down the other side. Tall mountains surrounded them. They were in high country now. The snow line wasn't far, just an hour's climb away.

The lofty summits beckoned Aditya. The mountains called out to him, flaunting their challenge. Their upper reaches were sacred, they seemed to say, only for the brave. Did he have the courage, they wanted to know? Did he have the strength, the spirit or the character to climb them? Aditya experienced a deep urge to strike out for the peaks, but Tsering's presence held him back.

Tsering chattered suddenly, pointing to the mountainside opposite. Looking up, Aditya spotted what the boy had seen.

Marmots!

Whipping out his binoculars, Aditya trained them on the slope. The marmots had seen the boys and were scurrying for cover. Aditya laughed. Marmot locomotion is comical. The animals are fat balls of fur. Their movements are funny indeed: a kind of rolling, twisting motion, more like a frantic waddle.

A few of the furry animals stood their ground. The rest disappeared into the earth. Marmots live in burrows, which they escape into at the first sign of danger. Aditya was familiar with marmots, having seen them earlier on the grasslands of Tso Kar. Their burrows were everywhere on the rolling plain. The little animals had fascinated both him and Vikram and they had never tired of watching them.

The slope on which the marmots stood was green— not a patchy green, but a lush, delightful green. So these were the summer pastures that the shepherds migrated to. When Meme Chacko had spoken about the pastures, Aditya had found it difficult to believe him. Ladakh was a desert. That was what he had been told, and all that he had seen of it confirmed what he had heard. If the lower slopes were barren, then how could the upper slopes be green? But Meme Chacko was right, the evidence was there before his eyes. In addition to the green, Aditya's binoculars picked out patches of yellow too. Not only was there grass but also flowers.

This was a nice place to spend the rest of the day. Tsering did not seem to mind when Aditya unhitched his pack. They searched the slope and finding a truck-sized boulder that blocked the rays of the sun, they settled themselves in its shade.

Transcript of radio conversation at noon

Vikram: All well with you? Over.

Aditya: Yeah, no problem. [*pause*] Vikram, remember Meme Chacko telling us about those green pastures, the ones high on the mountain slopes? I didn't believe him then, but there's one right opposite me and I tell you, it's green. The view from here is stunning. Tsering and I have been passing time, trying to converse. I've been teaching him Hindi. He's an intelligent sort, picking up whatever I say. Here, he wants to talk to you. Over.

Tsering: *Aap kaise hai*, Vikram?

Vikram [*in Hindi*]: I'm fine and how are you, Tsering?

Tsering: *Mein theek hoon, shukriya*.

Aditya: Not bad, huh? Check his vocabulary by evening. Tell me, what's happening at your end? Over.

Vikram: That jeep we saw entering Tso Kar is a tourist jeep, and it's parked next to our camp. Oddly, there's only one tourist in it, a Japanese gentleman with four helpers. Seems extravagant to me, four helpers, one man. They've set up two tents not far from ours. I went across to meet the man, but he speaks only Japanese. He was quite rude, making it clear he wasn't pleased with my presence, so I backed away leaving him to his business. He appears to be a dedicated birdwatcher. You should see his equipment—it's impressive and expensive too. The man has fancy binoculars, cameras with long lenses and a telescope. He's an odd fellow . . . Quite a character. Over.

Aditya: Scare the birds away! Make sure he has none to watch. That ought to teach him manners. Over!

Vikram [*laughing*]: I was thinking of taking Nanju's boom box out and blasting it by the lakefront. [*pause*] Our Tibetan friends are at the same place; no movement at their end. Nothing else to report, I'll call you after an hour. Over and out.

Transcript of radio conversation at 1.15 p.m.

Vikram: Hi Aditya, can you hear me? Over.

Aditya: Loud and clear, Vikram. Listen, I spotted a man with horses just after talking to you. He was crossing a valley not far from here. I left Tsering behind and made my poor horse run again so I could intercept the man before the next pass. He told me he is a camp boy working for a pair of Swedish trekkers. They intend to camp at Tso Kar tonight. The Swedes are following behind with a guide. The man's job is to set up camp and prepare the evening meal for his sahibs. I plan to meet the trekkers and talk to them. What's happening at your end? Over.

Vikram: Nothing much. Our Japanese friend is a weird character all right. His pricey equipment is set-up on the lakefront, but he isn't using it. He spends his time in his tent instead. His men too are all in their tents. Over.

Aditya: Maybe he's suffering from altitude sickness. How's Nanju? Over.

Vikram: He's okay, bored I guess, like me. There isn't much to do at camp. I'll probably ride to Tso Kar sometime later to watch the birds. Over.

Aditya: You watch birds, my friend. I'm up here in snow leopard territory. Guess what I'll find while you stare at your birds? Over.

Vikram: You're dreaming as usual, Aditya. I'll call you later. Over and out.

Transcript of radio conversation at 2 p.m.

Vikram: So, have you found a snow leopard? Over.

Aditya: Have patience, my friend. I'll get to the snow leopard part later, but listen to this first. Just a while back, Tsering and I saw a big bird circling low over the mountains. It was brown, the biggest I've ever seen, and its neck was golden. I clearly saw the gold feathers through my binoculars. I am sure it was a golden eagle. Ha, ha, Vikram, I saw a golden eagle. Eat your heart out. And there's more. We watched him fly in low, skimming at slope level. The marmots didn't notice him till he was over their colony. Then all hell broke loose. There was panicked chattering and the hillside exploded into motion, marmots scrambling everywhere. The eagle had targeted a fat specimen, and while he frantically waddled away, the bird struck. The force of the strike was tremendous, and the poor creature went bowling over. By the time it recovered, the bird had landed on it. I thought the marmot was a goner, but somehow, just as the bird reached down with its beak, the animal broke free. There must have been a burrow nearby because the fat marmot disappeared in an instant. The entire hillside was suddenly empty. There wasn't a single animal to be seen. Over.

Vikram: Yes, the bird must have been a golden eagle. You lucky dog! Over.

Aditya: Wait, I haven't finished. Almost immediately after the eagle flew away, I saw this snow-white animal with grey spots. Over.

Vikram: I'm sure you did, Aditya. You know, what you say makes perfect sense, because five snow leopards visited our camp an hour ago. Nanju fed them lunch and then shooed them away. One of them headed towards the same pass you had climbed. That was probably the animal you saw. Over.

Aditya [*laughing*]: Okay, okay, but just you wait, I will spot a snow leopard today. They are bound to be here somewhere in this high country. [*pause*] Tsering and I have descended into the next valley. We hope to meet the Swedes here. In the meanwhile, we are going to continue with our Hindi lessons. What's happening at your end? Over.

Vikram: Nothing exciting, I'm leaving for Tso Kar now. I'll call you after two hours. Over and out.

Vikram spent the afternoon by the lake watching birds. Though the white waters of Tso Kar were not fit for drinking, the fish managed to survive in them. And because of the fish, there were birds in plenty. Vikram saw redshanks, greenshanks, sand plovers, river terns and Brahminy ducks. There were seagulls too, and their presence surprised him. The birds were identical to the gulls that he had seen along the beaches of Mumbai and Goa. What were gulls doing here, he wondered? Didn't seagulls live only by the sea?

It was a warm and pleasant afternoon. Vikram had his bird books with him, and he referred to them often, identifying birds he hadn't seen before. Tso Kar was an excellent site for water birds and Vikram soon forgot about the kidnappers.

Transcript of radio conversation at 4 p.m.

Vikram: So, how many snow leopards have you seen, Aditya? Over.

Aditya: Have patience! I'll find one. I've found humans here instead. The Swedish couple have shown up, and I've been chatting with them. I was hesitant to start with . . . you know . . . talking about our problems, but they are really nice people—thank God for that—and it all came out as we talked. Their names are Anders and Eva Lindgren—not your typical tourists as they actually live here in India, in Pune. The important thing is that they are willing to help us. They've invited Tsering and me to spend the night with them at their camp. That is what I was hoping for, and it solves our problem for the night. Also, a vehicle is coming in for them from Leh. The driver will spend the night with them and take them back to Leh tomorrow. That's perfect for us, isn't it? Because if the kidnappers are still hanging around in the morning, we can leave with Anders and Eva and return to Leh. What do you think? Over.

Vikram [*long pause*]: Yes, it's a good idea, staying with your Swedish friends. I had started to worry about the night. No other tourists have arrived, and judging by the way the Japanese man is behaving, I don't think he'll be of any help. Spend the night with your Swedish friends, but be careful, no one should see you enter the valley. Sneak in only after dark. I can see their campsite from where I am. There are three tents pitched beside the Changpa settlement. A man came in with horses some time ago. I'm certain he's the camp boy you met earlier. So the Changpa settlement will be your campsite for the night. Should I call you around eight? Over.

Aditya: Yes, eight should be fine. Don't worry, I'll enter the valley after dark.

We have time to kill here. We'll occupy
ourselves searching for a snow leopard. I'm
sure I'll find one . . . Any bets? Over.

Vikram [*laughed loudly*]: Best of luck,
O great tracker of the Himalayan ghost.
Call you later. Over and out.

Vikram did not spot the cranes again. But their absence
didn't trouble him, as there was plenty of birdlife on the
lake. He saw bar-headed geese—birds he greatly admired.
These big swan-sized birds were exceptionally strong
fliers. His father had told him that they had been seen
migrating across the Himalayas at 25,000 feet, far higher
than other birds can fly. Vikram had spotted the geese
often on the plains of north India—but always during the
winter. This was the first time he had seen the birds in
their summer home.

Vikram feasted his eyes on gulls, terns, geese, waders
and ducks. The birds were delightful to watch, yet he
was in no doubt that here on Tso Kar, the tall and stately
cranes were the most majestic of all. Big, in their case, was
truly beautiful.

Towards the evening, Vikram heard piercing calls
from the far side of the lake. He listened, mesmerized.
Never had he heard such wild and haunting sounds. The
cranes . . . it had to be them. This was their unison call.
Vikram pictured the birds standing at full height, their
feathers fluffed, ripping their booming calls skywards.
A poet had described their call as 'the trumpet in the

orchestra of evolution'. On the lonely plateau of Tso Kar, with the strains of their primeval song ringing across the wilderness, Vikram couldn't agree more.

As the melody of the cranes' song faded, Vikram was struck by a disturbing thought. It was clear from his experience on the lake that each of the various species of birds here were represented by several hundred individuals. But in the case of the cranes, there was just one family. If the dog had succeeded in killing the baby crane, three individuals would have been reduced to two.

Meme Chacko had kept watch over twelve nests the previous year and had counted twenty-one eggs. From those, only four chicks had survived. It wasn't just that the crane population was low; even the survival rate of their hatchlings was threatened. Vikram now understood why the cranes were considered so rare and endangered.

This lone family of cranes added grace and character to Tso Kar. Vikram had witnessed the nimble, smooth power of their flight and had heard their magnificent unison call. But would the cranes be here the next time he visited? It would indeed be a sad day if the cranes were to disappear from here forever. The lakes would never be the same if their calls fell silent.

IN THE DEAD OF THE NIGHT

Vikram trotted his horse across the grass plain, returning to his camp before sunset. The sun shone brightly, embracing him with welcome warmth. The sky was mostly blue except for a solitary black cloud that hung motionless overhead.

Visibility was perfect, and Vikram had an excellent view of the entire basin. He experienced a faint sense of disappointment as he looked around him. Tourists had not flocked to Tso Kar as he had hoped. Three camps was the final count for the evening. His own camp was visible on the shores of Tsa Tsa Phuk Tso. Beside it were pitched the tents of the Japanese birdwatcher. In the distance, hidden in the shadow of the mountains, was the Swedish trekkers' camp. The kidnappers hadn't given up and gone home. Like wolves biding their time, they lurked on the plain, their vehicle parked on the far side of the lakes.

There was not a breath of wind. The basin was vast and empty, a picture of unspoilt wilderness. The snow on the mountains flashed gold in the rays of the setting sun. The temperature was the warmest it had been throughout the day. But in spite of the near-perfect conditions, the solitary cloud above prompted Vikram to urge his horse faster. Slender fingers of white trailed beneath the cloud. Vikram didn't know whether to feel foolish as he sped his horse forward. Was he being overcautious? Yet he urged his mount on, galloping to the camp. The white tracers caught him just as he reached the tents.

Ice!

The slanting white trailers were sleet! Vikram dashed to his tent and dived between the flaps. Sleet pounded the campsite and drummed against the nylon fabric of his shelter.

The view from the tent was unreal. Warm sunshine continued to flood the basin while curtains of ice, flashing in the sun, smothered the campsite. To the east, at the base of the mountains, a rainbow arched heavenward. The sleet stopped as abruptly as it had arrived, and the cloud drifted to the mountains, trailing a glistening wake. The entire episode lasted barely two minutes.

The Japanese birdwatcher's expensive cameras and telescopes had remained outside during the downpour. As the rainbow faded, the man emerged from his tent, but instead of rushing to his cameras, he walked away to the lake. Vikram found his attitude astonishing. All that wonderful equipment pummelled by ice and rain and the man wasn't even bothered. Was he really a birdwatcher? If he was, then he was certainly the strangest birdwatcher Vikram had ever seen.

Later, as the light started to fade, a truck appeared in the basin and crossed between the lakes. Motoring past

Vikram's camp, it halted at the Swedes' camp. Shortly after sunset, as the western sky turned gold, the kidnappers' jeep finally moved. It turned away from Vikram's camp and drove towards Tso Kar. Not travelling far, the vehicle halted and doused its lights.

Light lingered in the sky for a long time, and when the night chill descended, Vikram retreated to the kitchen tent where he was served a delicious hot meal. Meme Chacko had always maintained that he couldn't have stayed away from home for such long periods had it not been for Nanju and the authentic south Indian food he cooked. Sure enough, the sambar, rice and vegetables Nanju had put together were of a high standard—one that even Vikram's late mother would have approved of.

Nanju was a pleasant young man who loved the company of friends and enjoyed exchanging gossip, even with strangers. 'Those people—' he said, while Vikram dug appreciatively into his meal, '—those helpers of the Japanese man . . . They are strange people. Very rude.' There was hurt in the cook's voice.

Vikram looked up.

'Those men were playing cards in the afternoon,' went on Nanju. 'I was free with nothing to do, so I went across to join them. They refused to let me play, and they spoke roughly to me, asking me to go away. Those men are not from here, Vikram sahib. They are not from Ladakh. They are Tibetan, just like the men who tried to kidnap Tsering.'

Vikram stopped eating. Tibetan? Tsering had pointed to Tibet when he'd described the people who had tried to kidnap him. His kidnappers were Tibetans, Chinese Tibetans.

'Nanju, are these men Chinese Tibetans or Tibetan refugees who live in India?'

Nanju thought for a while and then shook his head. 'I cannot say, sir,' he admitted. 'I do not know.'

Vikram retired to his tent after dinner. The glow in the west had dimmed and stars twinkled above. It was cold outside, and Vikram quickly buried himself inside the folds of his sleeping bag. When he was warm and cosy, he switched on his radio.

Aditya's voice crackled cheerfully through the handset.

'Hi Vikram, can you believe it, the cook here can make Italian food! We had a fab pasta dinner. You should have seen Tsering. That kid wolfed it down. Jealous, huh? Bet you are. All is well at our end. There is a truck parked here; you must have seen it drive in earlier. It's come for the Swedes, to take them back to Leh. Do you think we should leave with Anders and Eva tomorrow? They are fine with taking us along with them. Over.'

'You and Tsering go with them, Aditya. I'd rather stay with Nanju and wait for Meme Chacko. Tsering's safety is important, so you should go to Leh. Over.'

'We'll decide about that tomorrow. How are our kidnapper friends? Over.'

'They finally moved about an hour ago and are parked now somewhere near Tso Kar. They have no clue that you are at the Swedes' camp. They probably think that you will return here during the night. They'll keep a sharp watch on our camp, and I expect a visit from them sometime tonight. Over.'

'Do you think they'll attack the camp? Over.'

'Not really. They don't care about me, they want Tsering. Over.'

'Well, look after yourself. Call me . . . No, wait. I'll call you. How does 5 a.m. sound? Over.'

'At sunrise? Over,' asked Vikram incredulously.

'Yeah.' There was resignation in Aditya's voice. 'That's the time these Swedes wake up. Over.'

'What a wonderful change to have you wake me up. I look forward to that, Aditya. Goodnight. Over.'

'Goodnight, Vikram, and take care. Over and out.'

Vikram switched off his radio. In the silence that followed, he heard a faint sound. A quiet rustle, like something brushing against the grass. Was there somebody outside his tent? It couldn't be the kidnappers. Their jeep had been parked at Tso Kar, many kilometres away. But then who could it be? Was someone eavesdropping on his conversation with Aditya? Vikram did not have time to think. The tent flaps were rudely jerked apart, and a jumble of shadows tumbled inside.

Vikram's voice failed him. His lips twitched fervently, yet no sound emerged. Someone grabbed his sleeping bag and tugged with considerable force. Trapped inside its zippered confines, Vikram was dragged helplessly through the flaps and dumped on the grass outside. His fingers scrabbled desperately for the zip, and locating it, he managed to jerk it down a few inches. Vikram tugged again, but the slider snagged on the cloth. Sleeping bags are not designed for rapid exits, and poor Vikram stood no chance. There were four men surrounding him, and though he struggled, his energies were confined within the bag. The men easily overpowered him, and he was soon yanked out of the bag. A rough, wet rope was wound tightly around his wrists and legs.

~f

Tsering had been unhappy with the decision to return to Tso Kar. He had tried to communicate his displeasure, but Aditya had shrugged him off, pointing to their Swedish friends in a manner that suggested that they would protect them during the night.

Tsering was afraid of returning to the lakes. Even though they had crept into the Swedes' camp in complete darkness, Tsering was certain that the kidnappers would find him there. Only Tsering understood the resolve of the men. He knew that the men were not alone, that they were part of a team, a team that had been relentlessly pursuing him for weeks. Poor Tsering. He had tried hard to convey the seriousness of the matter to Aditya, but the language barrier had defeated him. It was against his wishes that he had followed Aditya into Tso Kar.

A special tent had been erected for Aditya and Tsering, but Tsering had refused to sleep in it. When Tsering dragged his sleeping bag out of the tent, Aditya had tried to stop him, but the young Tibetan had been firm about not sleeping in the tent, and Aditya had let the matter drop.

Instead, Tsering chose to spend the night in the truck that was to take the Swedes back to Leh. There was ample space in the cargo section, and Tsering had spread his sleeping bag on its steel floor. Tsering's uneasiness prevented him from falling asleep, and despite his fatigue from the day's exertions, he lay awake in the truck.

The sound of footsteps in the dead of the night disturbed Tsering. His breath quickened. The footsteps were slow and measured and were heading for the truck. The cargo section, where Tsering was stretched out, wasn't locked. The rear door was down and Tsering could see stars through the opening. The stars were abruptly snuffed out by shadows. Tsering froze, his breathing coming in halting gasps. He counted the shadows. Three, four . . . and a fifth one. Five shadows crept soundlessly into the camp. The kidnappers. Tsering didn't doubt for a moment that it was them. The shadows spread out in the camp, making for the tents. Tsering was zipped tightly in his sleeping bag, but he dared not unzip it. So still was the night that Tsering held his breath, frightened that even that tiny sound might alert the men.

Tsering waited. The silence was ruptured by the sound of ripping fabric and the thump of running feet. Taking advantage of the commotion, Tsering unzipped his bag. Crawling to the edge of the cargo bay, he jumped to the ground and slid under the truck.

In spite of the absence of the moon, Tsering could see clearly. Every tent had been ripped out of the ground.

Nylon fabric, aluminium poles, rucksacks and water bottles lay in a tangled mess. There was vigorous squirming and thumping from under the mess, and the kidnappers stood in a ring around the upturned pile. Tsering did not linger. No one was looking in his direction. Crouching low, the little boy fled.

A mountain stream flowed behind the camp. Tsering dropped behind a waist-high ledge to the sandy bank of the stream. He was safe, but only for the moment. The kidnappers would soon realize he was missing, and a search would be launched.

Tsering had to find a place to hide. Across the stream, the shadowed Changpa settlement was visible. The stone huts offered a hiding place, but Tsering hesitated. The huts were an obvious hiding place. The abandoned village would be the first place the kidnappers would search. It was the only cover for miles around.

Tsering had to make a decision fast. If the Changpa settlement was too obvious, the stream bed could be a place they might overlook. Deciding on the stream bed, Tsering stooped low and scuttled downstream, running in the icy water. His feet quickly lost feeling, yet the boy persevered. After a few minutes of painful progress, Tsering finally halted. Crouching behind the sand embankment, he slowly raised his head and stared back at the camp.

Five erect shadows encircled a group of sitting shadows. Tsering counted the people who had been at the camp before the kidnappers had struck. There were the two Swedes, Aditya, two camp boys and the driver of the truck.

Squinting, Tsering tallied the shadows on the ground. There were six—all his friends had been captured.

The kidnappers were upset. They were shouting and waving their arms. Tsering grinned. There was no doubt it was his absence they were discussing. Tsering was of the opinion that he had travelled a safe distance from the camp. It was unlikely that the men would come searching for him here; they would search the abandoned village first.

Tsering's guess was correct. Three men soon set off for the settlement. Crossing the stream, they dispersed amongst the huts. Flashlights pinpointed their locations as they methodically searched each dwelling.

Tsering longed to escape to the mountains. He was confident he could elude the kidnappers there. He felt trapped on the grasslands. There was no place to hide, and if he attempted to flee, the men would run him down in their jeep. Yet, Tsering was sensible enough to realize that there was no hope of getting to the mountains. There was no option for the moment. He would have to wait where he was.

Tsering's thoughts were disturbed by the sound of a vehicle. Lights were visible in the distance. A vehicle was moving on the plain, heading for the Swedes' camp.

It was a long ten minutes before the vehicle arrived. The driver killed the engine, leaving the lights on. Two figures dismounted awkwardly from the rear door. It was evident from the way they walked that their hands were tied behind their backs. Vikram and Nanju! Tsering's head drooped. All his friends had been captured.

The kidnappers rerigged two of the tents in the glow of the headlights. The prisoners were crowded into the larger of the two. The men then settled themselves outside the smaller tent, resting on the ground.

Time passed. Stars crept across the sky, tracing their westward path across the heavens. After a while, a kidnapper, hunched beneath a load, crossed the stream and trekked to the Changpa settlement. It was only later that Tsering realized it was sleeping bags that the man was carrying. The men searching the village had decided to sleep there. Settling themselves along the edge of the settlement, they spread their bags on the ground. Tsering chuckled. This could only mean that the kidnappers believed he was holed up somewhere amidst the abandoned shelters.

The kidnappers soon turned in for the night. The arrival of the driver had added one more to their number. There were now six of them. Three were resting along the edge of the Changpa settlement, keeping guard there. The rest were at the Swedes' camp. One sat outside the large tent watching the prisoners. The remaining two had withdrawn to the smaller tent.

Tsering contemplated his next move. Spending the night by the stream wasn't a good idea. The men would come looking for him at first light, and they would surely find him there. Tsering had two choices: either make a break for the mountains or try and rescue his friends.

Tsering's conscience ruled out the mountains. Vikram and Aditya had not abandoned him when he had been kidnapped. They were in trouble now as a result. If at all he escaped, it would be with his friends. He would rescue them, but the time wasn't right.

Tsering waited.

ESCAPE

It grew colder as the night deepened. Tsering's Tibetan origins helped him bear the chill stoically. When the wet stream bank started crusting over with ice, Tsering chose to make his move. Keeping low, he crawled along the bank to the camp. When he drew close, he crept back above the ledge.

The tents stood before him. There was a man on sentry duty. He lay on the ground, tucked inside a sleeping bag at the entrance of the prisoners' tent. There was the sound of bells tinkling. Two packhorses, hobbled for the night, were picking at grass nearby.

The night was silent. The only other sound, besides that of the bells, was the murmur of running water. Tsering stared at the sentry. The man appeared to be asleep. There was no movement from his bag, except the rhythmic rise and fall of deep breathing.

Tsering was keenly aware he was visible to anybody who cared to look in his direction. The men sleeping on the far side of the stream bothered him the most. He couldn't see them, but if they woke and glanced across at the tents, they would surely see him. But Tsering had little choice. He could only pray that they were asleep.

Tsering had a plan. He needed a knife, and he knew where to find one. He had washed two sharp kitchen knives earlier and had laid them on a cloth to dry along with other utensils. The cloth had been spread behind the kitchen tent. The tent had since been pulled to the ground by the kidnappers. Tsering crept towards the uprooted tent and searched out the dinner utensils. The knives lay side by side amidst a clutter of plates, vessels and spoons. Tsering retrieved the knives and slid away towards the tents.

The smaller tent housed the sleeping kidnappers. Pitched to its right was the larger prisoners' tent. Tsering edged forward, his body parallel to the ground. He crawled to the prisoners' tent, to its far side, opposite the entrance flaps and the sleeping sentry. On reaching it, he gently rested his fingers on the tent's nylon surface.

Tsering's hands were clammy as he grasped one of the knives. On his knees, he pressed the knife through the fabric of the tent. There was a rustling inside followed by silence. Tsering worked fast, slitting a hole. Then gently pulling back the fabric, he stuck his head inside. His eyes took a while to adjust to the darkness inside the tent. At first, all he saw was shadows. Then the shadows took form and Tsering was able to discern faces, all of them smiling.

There was silence, not a word was spoken. The shadow to Tsering's right was Aditya's. Wasting no time, Tsering worked on the rope, binding the boy's hands. When Aditya was free, Tsering pressed the second knife into his hands.

The shout from outside was so sudden that Tsering's heart somersaulted in his chest. Everyone in the tent froze. The shout was repeated, a note of anger clearly discernible this time. Simultaneously, there was the jingling of bells and a snort. The packhorses! The sentry was shooing away a packhorse. The guard mumbled something at the animal and there was silence again.

It was a long time before Aditya and Tsering thought it safe to move again. They worked silently at the bonds of their friends, and in a short while, everybody was free. Vikram hugged Tsering in the darkness and the little boy squeezed his hand.

Anders, the Swede, was the first to crawl out of the hole Tsering had cut. Aditya moved to follow, but Anders stopped him. The Swede was firm and pushed Aditya back into the tent. Instead it was the truck driver whom Anders reached for. Holding the man's hand, Anders led him out.

Anders stuck his head back into the tent, signalling for the others to sit and wait. Then he withdrew and disappeared with the driver.

Vikram felt Aditya stir beside him. Reaching out, Vikram clamped down hard on his friend's hand. 'Wait!' he whispered. Aditya fidgeted but sat silently. When Anders returned a few minutes later, Aditya crawled out to meet him.

For a Swede, Anders wasn't particularly tall. The faint light outlined a strong-boned profile and his blonde hair flashed silver. On seeing Aditya, he pressed a finger to his lips. Turning, he beckoned Aditya to follow. Stepping quietly, he led Aditya past the kidnappers' tent to a jeep—the vehicle that had brought Vikram and Nanju to the camp. Its door was open. Slipping inside, Anders made space for Aditya on the front seat.

Anders whispered in accented English. 'Listen to me. We wanted to escape in the truck, but the keys were taken from the driver when they captured us. Luckily, the keys to this jeep have been left in the ignition.' The Swede paused. 'Look there,' he said softly, pointing to the truck parked a few metres away. 'Our driver is inside the truck. He's sabotaging his own vehicle, cutting the fuel lines and ignition wires. He will be done soon. By then I intend to have everyone in the jeep. The plan is simple. We sabotage all vehicles and drive away in this jeep. You stay here inside the jeep. I'll bring the others one by one.'

Anders did not give Aditya an opportunity to reply. Squeezing his shoulder, he dropped soundlessly to the ground.

Aditya had taken a liking to Anders and Eva from the moment they had met. Now, as he watched Anders pad soundlessly to the tents, his respect for the Swede grew further. It had only been a few hours since Anders and Eva had met him. Yet they hadn't complained even once about the troubles he and Tsering had inflicted on them. In fact, it was Anders who had fought most fiercely when their tents had been ripped out of the ground, quitting only when a gun had been thrust in his face.

The prisoners began to arrive quickly, one by one, each accompanied by Anders. Tsering came first with a big grin on his face. Next was Eva, then Nanju, the cook. But after Nanju, their luck faltered.

Sounds rang from the Changpa settlement.

The tramp of marching feet filled the cold night air.

Anders was at the tent, crouched at the hole Tsering had cut when he heard the noise. Aware that he was visible to anyone at the settlement, he leapt into the tent.

In the jeep, Aditya heard the sounds too.

'Oh no,' murmured Eva, who was sitting beside Aditya.

A man was walking from the settlement to the camp. The abundant starlight of Tso Kar outlined his figure. He was making for the stream, and when he reached it, he switched on his torch, searching for a spot to ford it.

Aditya bit his lip. The man's presence was going to wreck their plans. The hole Tsering had cut faced the direction from which he was approaching. The man would have to be blind not to notice it.

Acting on impulse, Aditya dropped from the jeep to the ground. Turning, he faced the torchlight. The man was still searching for a place to cross the stream. There was time. If he was quick, Aditya could make it to the tents. Keeping low, he scampered towards them.

Aditya approached from the side where the sentry slept. He had no choice, as the tents provided the only cover between him and the man crossing the stream. A packhorse grazing nearby backed away noisily when Aditya raced past it. He grimaced and kept running. Aditya sacrificed stealth for speed. On hands and knees, he crawled to the small tent—the one with the sleeping kidnappers—

and crouched beside it. Aditya's dash to the tent hadn't woken the sentry. The man slept undisturbed outside the prisoners' tent. Mindful of the sleeping man, Aditya edged to the side of the tent and peered at the stream.

The kidnapper from the settlement had crossed the stream and was climbing the ledge. His torch beam flashed on the shadowed ground as he walked towards the tents.

Aditya backed off behind the small tent and waited.

The torch swung forward and illuminated the prisoners' tent. The footsteps stopped. Aditya heard a sharp intake of breath followed by the sound of running feet.

The sentry was stirring. There was movement inside the kidnappers' tent too.

Aditya stuck his head round the tent, looking directly at the kidnapper, who was sprinting now. The tent seemed to quiver when the kidnapper halted at the hole Tsering had cut. A shadow shot out from within. It was Anders, and his leap propelled him head first on to the man.

The small tent was shaking violently. The sentry was awake and tugging frantically at the zip of his sleeping bag. The flaps of the prisoners' tent were thrust aside, and a shadow lunged forward, landing squarely on the sentry. Aditya waved his fist in glee when he saw a second shadow tumble out from the flaps. The sentry had his hands full.

Aditya was conscious of the presence of a gun. It was a short man with long, curly hair who had brandished the weapon at them, quelling all resistance earlier. Hand-to-hand tussles were not going to decide this encounter.

The possession of the weapon would be the deciding factor. Aditya crouched at the entrance of the smaller tent. Was the curly-haired man inside?

The flaps were flung aside, and a man emerged. Aditya, who was about to leap, held back. It wasn't the curly-haired man. Aditya restrained himself as he watched the man run to the aid of the sentry. One more occupant remained within the tent. It had to be the curly-haired man.

A free-for-all was in progress outside the large tent. The sentry, still hampered by his sleeping bag, was being held down by one of Anders' camp boys. The second camp boy was grappling with the man who had leapt out of the small tent. Another encounter was taking place behind, between Anders, Vikram and the man whose presence had started the skirmish.

The flaps beside Aditya were thrust aside and a curly-haired head popped out. Aditya saw the gun. It was grasped in the man's left hand. The man's attention was focused on the wrestling figures outside the large tent. He had no idea of the danger lurking beside him, and when Aditya leapt on him, he was thoroughly taken by surprise.

Aditya landed on the man as he was rising to his feet. He reached out for the hand that held the gun. In a purely reflex action, the curly-haired man's finger closed convulsively on the trigger. There was a loud report as the gun went off.

Vikram jumped like a startled rabbit. Anders reacted with alarm too, almost letting go of the man he held. Looking up they saw Aditya, the curly-haired man and the gun.

Aditya was far bigger than his adversary. His left hand held the gun hand of the smaller man in an unshakeable grip. Aditya was working on the man's hand, exerting all his considerable strength.

Satisfied that Aditya had the man in control, Vikram concentrated on the fight at hand. Anders did not require any help, having easily overpowered his opponent. But reinforcements for the kidnappers were on their way. Two figures were sprinting towards them from the settlements.

Aditya bodily lifted the curly-haired man and threw him to the ground. He repeated the manoeuvre once again and then clamped down on the gun hand with all his strength. Vikram saw the gun fall from the man's hand. Shouting encouragement to Aditya, he ran forward and scooped the weapon from the ground.

Anders saw Vikram grab the gun. He too had spotted the approaching reinforcements. Time was running out. Anders bunched his fist and swung it with all his strength at his opponent's stomach. Gasping, the man doubled over. For good measure, Anders let him have one more.

There was the sound of an engine coming to life. Bright headlights illuminated the tents. Anders saw that Aditya did not require assistance. The curly-haired man was trapped beneath him. But his camp boys needed help. Thrusting aside his subdued opponent, the Swede ran towards them.

The jeep rolled forward, driving towards the tents. The two men from the settlement had reached the stream. Not aiming directly at them, Vikram pointed the gun in their direction and fired. Both came to a halt, one diving to the ground. The second man leapt for cover too when Vikram fired once more.

Events unfolded rapidly thereafter, and Vikram wasn't able to properly recollect their sequence later. Shooting live bullets had a trance-like effect on him. Although Vikram was familiar with weapons, he had never shot at anybody before. He recollected later that the headlights of the jeep had blinded him. Then somebody had yanked at his shirt, shouting, 'Come on!'

The kidnappers were a thoroughly subdued lot. Anders had flattened one of them, Aditya had thrashed the curly-haired man and the others had given up when they discovered that Vikram had seized the gun.

Aditya was the last to board the jeep and the driver accelerated powerfully. Aditya wanted to stop by their camp at Tsa Tsa Phuk Tso to collect their belongings, but Anders refused. The Swede was in no mood to linger. The priority was to get away from the kidnappers as rapidly as possible.

There was hardly any jubilation in the jeep. Their violent, hard-fought victory had drained them. They were tired, cold and frightened. In quick time, they drove out between the lakes and ascended the Polokong La pass. Dorje and his people slept as the jeep roared past their reebos.

Their first halt was Sumdo, the tiny settlement where Vikram and Aditya had met Tsering. The dark of the night had yielded to the flush of morning by the time they arrived. In spite of the early hour, the school quadrangle was abuzz with activity. They were ushered to the headmaster's office and served mugs of steaming tea.

The headmaster, an elderly man with thick spectacles, listened with a worried look while Vikram narrated their story. But his face turned blank when on completing his story, Vikram asked about Tsering.

The headmaster was courteous but firm. He apologized, saying he could not talk about the boy or the kidnappers. Instead he requested them to hurry on with their journey to Leh. 'Tsering is not safe here,' he explained. 'The kidnappers are desperate men, and they will attack the school if we keep him here.' He requested that a teacher from the school accompany them. The man would take care of Tsering at Leh and deliver him to a 'safe' house.

Later, the headmaster made one final request. 'I know this is difficult, but I must insist. Please, please do not tell anybody about what took place at Tso Kar. No police, nobody! Meme Chacko swore you to secrecy,' he reminded the boys. 'Now I beg the same of all of you. Don't ask for reasons, just believe in me. Please give me your word. I assure you, thousands of people will be eternally grateful to you for doing so.'

The headmaster looked at each one of them in turn.

Anders shrugged. 'I don't care, it makes no difference to me,' he said.

Eva smiled and hugged Tsering. 'For this little boy, I will promise anything,' she said.

Vikram, Aditya, Nanju, the guides and the driver all promised to keep the encounter at Tso Kar a secret.

When Vikram mentioned that their luggage was still at Tso Kar, the headmaster promised to have everything collected for them. Meme Chacko would be passing through Sumdo on his return. The headmaster would request him to collect their belongings.

It was decided that Nanju and the two camp boys would not travel to Leh. They would wait at the school for Meme Chacko. Vikram, Aditya, the Swedes, Tsering, his escort the schoolteacher and the driver would all proceed to Leh.

Before leaving, Tsering indulged everyone with a tour of the school, introducing them to his friends and teachers. Vikram had been impressed with the school on his first visit itself. The classrooms were neat and tidy, and their walls were painted with bright, eye-catching colours. The children were happy and well looked after. There was determination in the eyes of the teachers, warmth in the attitude of the headmaster and a sense of purpose amongst the children. It was remarkable that a school of this calibre flourished in such a remote location. Ladakh, thought Vikram as they drove away, was full of surprises.

LEH

In the southern reaches of the massive Changthang plateau of Tibet lies the sacred mountain Kailash and its emerald lake, Manasarovar. Mount Kailash is famous not just because it is a holy place but also because the highlands that surround it are the birthplace of some of Asia's greatest rivers, including the Indus and the Brahmaputra. But surprisingly, though these two mighty rivers have an almost identical source, they flow in opposite directions. For the Brahmaputra, after a journey of many thousands of kilometres, its final destination is the Bay of Bengal. The Indus drains itself on the other side of the Indian subcontinent, into the Arabian Sea.

Flowing north across the Changthang plateau of Tibet, the Indus enters India at Ladakh. Cutting through the heart of this northern district, it then flows into Kashmir and from there into Pakistan. The river is fast-flowing and smooth near Leh where it rushes across a wide plain. But in the mountainous region east of Leh, the river is often a noisy torrent, frothing and foaming as it sweeps through narrow valleys and deep gorges.

The road from Tso Kar to Leh runs along the Indus, following the tortuous route the river has cut for itself through the Ladakh Range. The jeep carrying Vikram and his friends travelled this road, crossing the river often, switching sides via shaky suspension bridges. Although Vikram had not slept a wink the previous night, the fearsome beauty of the landscape energized his drooping eyelids, ensuring his wakefulness through the entire journey.

Having left the Changthang plateau behind, the road entered a range of barren, desolate mountains. Vikram saw boulders everywhere, varying in size from tiny rocks to gigantic ones as large as apartment blocks. It was as if someone possessing a vast collection of them had dumped them on the land. There were boulders on the mountains, boulders on the road and boulders in the deep gorge of the river.

The mountains soared above them, some snow-capped, others bare. Enormous slopes reached skyward, often covered with a loose, crumbling material, which somehow clung to their steeply inclined surface. These were scree slopes and Vikram soon discovered that they were a regular feature of the Ladakh landscape.

In a chameleon-like manner, the mountains kept changing colours. In some sections, they were shaded brown; in others, they were purple—sometimes they appeared orange and sometimes golden. It was a grand wilderness they drove through, hostile and inhospitable, yet magnificent to behold. Sheer mountainsides; windswept peaks; boulder-strewn slopes; tonnes of delicately balanced scree; twisting gorges; a frothing river—the images piled one upon the other, moving Vikram deeply, evoking in him a profound sense of desolation.

But Ladakh has a habit of springing surprises. In what often appeared to be the most appalling and dreadful terrain, patches of intense green would appear on barren mountainsides. The road would round a corner and Vikram would suddenly be confronted with carefully terraced fields, strings of fluttering prayer flags, flat-roofed houses and stands of poplar trees. The settlements were mostly small, restricted to just two or three houses. These tiny communities were few and far between, and the only other human presence was that of the Indian army with occasional outposts along the road.

The gorge of the Indus widened into a valley as it approached Leh. Villages began to appear frequently, and soon water flowed alongside the road in cemented irrigation canals. On some stretches of tree-lined roads, surrounded by fields, Vikram could swear that he was driving through lush alpine country. For those brief periods, it seemed ridiculous to call Ladakh a desert. But then suddenly, the fields and trees would disappear, the mountains would turn barren and sand dunes would appear.

The schoolteacher from Sumdo requested the driver to halt before Leh at the village of Choglamsar. Anders and Eva bid a drowsy goodbye to Tsering. Vikram and Aditya hugged the boy, not wanting to let him go. But the teacher was in a hurry. He promised them that this was not their final goodbye; they would meet Tsering again.

The boys were staying at the tiny Changspa Lodge in Leh. The driver drove them to its tucked-away location in the upper reaches of Leh city. Eva kissed both the boys and Anders shook hands with them. Deciding on a place to meet later that evening, the Swedes then drove away.

After every extended camping trip, the one thing Vikram eagerly looked forward to was a long shower. Retrieving their bags from the hotel manager, Aditya and he lingered under invigorating streams of steaming water. Then, after a hurried meal, they fell into deep slumber.

The boys had decided to meet Anders and Eva at a restaurant called Little Italy. Located centrally, it was a rooftop restaurant famous for the view from its upper deck, —an excellent panorama of the mountains surrounding Leh. It was evening and there was not a cloud in the sky. The sun was setting, the weather was warm and pleasant. To the south, the snow-capped peaks of the Zanskar Range burnt a warm orange in the slanting rays of the sun; and to the north, the brown peaks of the Ladakh Range brooded silently in the darkening sky.

Vikram, Aditya and their friends sat at a table alongside a railing, overlooking the busy street below. Anders and Eva were there, both scrubbed clean and looking relaxed. In addition to the Swedes, two young girls were also at the table, both friends of Aditya. The taller, dark-complexioned girl was Reena. Her father, Air Marshal Bhonagiri, was in charge of the air force station at Leh. The air marshal was an old friend of Aditya's father, and Aditya had known Reena since childhood.

Next to Reena sat her friend Dolma, a Ladakhi girl with high cheekbones and a slim, attractive face. The rooftop restaurant was owned by Dolma's father.

Engrossed in the mountain panorama, Vikram only paid half-attention as Anders spoke in his rumbling, accented voice. 'We should be leaving tomorrow,' the muscular Swede said, as he sipped coffee. 'I checked our bicycles and they are in good shape.'

'Our bicycles may be in good shape, but I'm not,' said Eva, laughing. She directed a meaningful look at her husband. 'I need at least two days' rest before such a difficult trip.'

'Bicycle trip?' Vikram spoke blankly, having no idea what they were talking about.

'Sorry, we never got a chance to tell you, did we?' Eva smiled. Her hair was golden in the evening sun and her blue eyes matched the colour of her denim jacket. 'We spoke about the trip to Aditya. Our Tso Kar trek was only the first part of our holiday. The next leg is a cycling trip to Taglang La. It won't be easy, far more difficult than our hike. Those days spent trekking at Tso Kar have tired me, and unlike Anders, I need a few days' rest.'

Aditya was in a prankish mood. He eyed Anders. The Swede's powerful build had impressed him from the moment they had met. For the heck of it, he decided to challenge his friend. 'You might be tough competition, Anders. You know, you are strong, well built. But I believe I can race you. If I were coming along, I'm sure I would reach the pass first.'

75

The Swede did not respond to Aditya's challenge. He simply smiled instead.

'Where is Taglang La?' inquired Vikram.

Dolma answered. 'Taglang La is the second highest motorable pass in the world at 17,500 feet. Khardung La, just north of here, is the highest. It is a few hundred feet higher.' Dolma was dressed in a pair of jeans and a white T-shirt. Her dark hair fell to her shoulders. Ladakhi girls were extremely attractive, but Dolma was by far the prettiest of all the girls Vikram had met in Leh. 'Nobody races up Taglang La,' she continued. 'The route is one of the toughest in the world and the final 3000 feet are a continuous climb—all up one mountain.'

'Three thousand feet up one mountain!' cried Eva. 'Heavens, Anders . . . You never told me about this.'

'It is hard work,' conceded Dolma, 'But you will manage, Eva, and so will Anders. But those who brag about racing up could get into trouble.'

Aditya shook his head. 'Tsk, tsk. Dolma here is jealous. Despite having lived all her sixteen years in Ladakh, she has never had the guts to attempt Taglang La, and so she runs down those who have the spirit to attempt it. Was I bragging, Anders, when I spoke of racing you?'

'No,' replied the Swede neutrally. Turning to Vikram, he changed the subject. 'Aditya was saying something about searching for the snow leopard and that the two of you are planning to join an expedition. It sounds interesting. What are your plans?'

Vikram pointed at the snow-capped peaks opposite. 'We should be headed there in a few days. Have you heard of an ecological group called Earthnet?'

The Swede shook his head.

'It's an international group that undertakes studies of endangered animals, and one of the projects it supports is the study of the snow leopard here in Ladakh. The study site is beyond those mountains. The chief investigator of the project is a wildlife scientist by the name of Dr Raghu Raman. He and my father are good friends. My father spoke to him, and he agreed to take us along.'

'Will you find a snow leopard?' asked Eva.

'I don't know,' answered Vikram truthfully.

'You mean you are going all the way up there and may not see any leopards?'

'We'll find them, Eva,' asserted Aditya confidently. 'At this time of the year, the leopards are in the high pastures following their prey, the bharal.* We will be camping in the pastures for two weeks; I'm sure we'll see one.'

Dolma sniggered.

Aditya glared at her.

For some reason, sparks always flew between the two of them. Aditya had first met Dolma the previous summer when his father was posted to Ladakh. Dolma's father, a prominent citizen of Leh, had struck up a friendship with Aditya's father. Dolma was a fiery young girl with a temperament similar to Aditya's, and although at first, the

---

* Also known as blue sheep

two of them had got along like favourite school chums, to the dismay of both sets of parents, their friendship had quickly crumbled, and the two had turned implacable foes. The antagonism continued, and even now, a year later, they never lost an opportunity to bait one another.

The anger in Aditya's eyes was all too evident as he spoke. 'Dolma's dad has often told me that he isn't pleased with the way the current crop of youngsters in Ladakh has turned out. He says Bollywood films, satellite TV and tourists have all had a damaging effect on Ladakhi youth. The youth, he says, have turned into city sorts, rejecting the outdoors and looking down on those who live off the land. He says they've lost the ability to suffer hardship and are rejecting the ways of the old. I didn't believe him then, but if you look at them—' he stared pointedly at Dolma, '—they don't wear traditional clothes any more. Instead they strut around in jeans, sport long earrings and put on lipstick and make-up. They behave like—'

Dolma banged her fist on the table, wrathfully interrupting Aditya. Her face glowed a flaming red, much like the evening sky. Her anger, thought Vikram, enhanced her considerable beauty.

'You, Aditya, are nothing but a big braggart! Race up Taglang La! Huh!' she exclaimed scornfully. 'Find snow leopards . . . What do you know about snow leopards? Your empty head is not going to help you find the animals. Greater men than you have searched and failed. And you, without any concept of what you are talking about, brag that you will find the animal.' Dolma spluttered, fizzing like an angry cat. 'What right do you have to speak about Ladakhi youth?'

Reena stared ashen-faced at Dolma.

Anders winked and made a face at Eva.

Vikram took a deep breath. He was familiar with Aditya's fierce outbursts. With bated breath, he waited for an explosion.

But unexpectedly, a calm fell upon Aditya. Speaking in a controlled voice, he addressed his friends. 'Please excuse me,' he said, rising from his seat. 'There is some work I have to complete. Anders, Eva, I will meet you tomorrow. Vikram, the plan is dinner at Alpha Mess with Reena's parents, right? I'll see you there at eight. Bye, Reena.'

Without waiting for a reply, Aditya strode to the stairs and descended to the street below. He pushed through the crowd, dodging tourists and vehicles. Aditya never walked away from a fight, and he hated himself for opting out, but he knew that if he had stayed on, he would have said things he would have regretted later.

The street teemed with people enjoying the evening sunshine. Tourists strolled along the sidewalks peering into shops. Cycles and vehicles plied the road. The 'work' he had spoken of—the motive for his abrupt departure—was a visit to a photo studio to print photos of their Tso Kar excursion. Aditya headed to a studio on Leh's High Street.

His ears pricked when he heard the chugging of a powerful motorcycle. He spotted a black Enfield cruising down the road. Astride it sat a stout blond-haired man and behind him a woman who had shaved her head bald.

Honking loudly, an army jeep with stern-faced soldiers in combat gear crossed them, driving in the opposite direction.

Posters of popular Hindi movies were displayed prominently at corners and on electricity poles. Shops and restaurants lined the sidewalks. If Aditya had not consumed a large slice of cake at the rooftop restaurant, he would definitely have entered the Mona Lisa German Bakery opposite, his favourite eatery in Leh. Rows of pastries, pies and cakes were visible through its glass frontage. Business was roaring. There was standing room only inside, and the tables that spilled on to the pavement were all occupied.

Summer was the time when tourists flocked to Leh. People of nationalities from across the world thronged the tiny street. Japanese, Americans, Russians, Israelis, Koreans and Europeans were some that Aditya recognized. Indians from the plains and uniformed jawans mingled with the local Ladakhis. Alien cultures rubbed shoulders comfortably. Young Ladakhi girls wore western clothes and western women wore Ladakhi clothes. Whacky fashions and colourful attire paraded before Aditya's eyes. The atmosphere on the street was carnival-like. Roadside vendors sold kathi kebabs and candyfloss. Eager shopkeepers hailed passing tourists, inviting them to view their wares.

Most of the tourists were young. Although not obvious, there was something different about them, thought Aditya. It showed in the way they dressed and in the carefree expressions on their faces. It was clear that they were not the five-star hotel type; rather they were a mix of the rugged, outdoor kind—wanderers with dreamy eyes who had come to seek the mountains.

Under the minarets of a large green mosque, Aditya turned on to Leh's High Street. The photo studio was adjacent to the mosque. A thin man behind the counter handed him a receipt and told him to collect the prints the next morning.

It was nearly half past seven. Though stars were asserting their presence in the sky, it was still warm, and it seemed that the entire population of Leh had turned out to enjoy a perfect summer evening. Aditya remembered his dinner engagement. Being a serviceman, Reena's father was a stickler for punctuality. The correct thing to do would be to head back to his hotel. But Aditya couldn't resist the lure of Leh's High Street. After the quiet, lonely nights at Tso Kar, the cheerful bustle of the street was too powerful an attraction to resist. Promising himself he would turn back in ten minutes, Aditya stepped on to the busy sidewalk.

Music and peals of merriment trickled from a restaurant named Himalayan Delights. Old men sat in chairs placed on the road, sucking deeply at their pipes. A young orange-robed boy smiled at Aditya as he walked past. His simple garment and shaven head announced he was a monk, but the elegant sunglasses slung around his neck and the fancy sneakers on his feet seemed to indicate otherwise. There were many monks, young and old, on the street. Though their neatly pressed robes were identical, some of the younger ones were distinctly fashion-conscious and sported all kinds of designer accessories.

Passing an antique shop with masks of a frowning Genghis Khan on display, Aditya suddenly halted. From the corner of his eye, he saw a plump, short man dressed in a blue shirt halt too. Aditya had first noticed the man with the blue shirt when he had paused opposite the bakery. It was the furtive glances he kept darting in his direction that had caught Aditya's attention. Later, when he had crossed the road to the photo studio, the man had crossed too. The man had waited a few shops down the street while Aditya finished his work and then had followed him again.

Aditya walked briskly forward, then turned abruptly, entering a shop that proudly called itself Ladakh Fashion Arcade. The shop was well-lit and there were customers inside. Pretending to take interest in a stand of T-shirts, Aditya asked the attendant if he had any 'Free Tibet' shirts. While the attendant searched, Aditya glanced at the door. The plump man had crossed the road. He stood on the pavement opposite, purchasing apricots from a roadside vendor.

The lights suddenly blacked out. Every shop on the street turned dark. There was a power failure across the city.

The attendant had found a shirt. 'Would you like to try this on?' he asked.

'No, thanks,' replied Aditya. 'I'll wait for the electricity to return. How long will that be?'

'Don't know, sir. The light comes and goes in the evening.'

'Some other time then,' said Aditya, smiling in the dark.

Aditya followed a group of German tourists to the door. Squeezing himself into their midst, he crouched as he stepped out of the shop. The entire street was in darkness. Aditya walked amongst the Germans. Ahead, he spotted another group of tourists. Slipping away from the Germans, he fell in with them.

The headlights of a bus driving down the road pierced the darkness. Aditya backed away, seeking the shadow of an overhanging display. The bus driver revved his engine warningly as he drove cautiously along the darkened road. The bus's headlights illuminated the plump man and Aditya saw him standing, apricots in hand, staring at the doorway of the shop he had exited. The vehicle passed Aditya. He waited till it travelled further, screening the plump man. When the man disappeared behind the bus, Aditya darted to the other side of the road. His ruse worked perfectly. The plump man had no idea he had crossed. He stood there in the darkness, gazing across the road.

Lanterns were being lit and power generators were cranking to life. Twinkling pools of light peeped out from restaurants and shops. The hustle and bustle of the street picked up again. Aditya stood next to a shop whose shutters were down. Though the darkness around him wasn't absolute, he was confident that the plump man would not be able to spot him. The power failure had reversed their roles. Now Aditya was the observer and his follower, the unwitting quarry.

The man sported a moustache. His expression was uncertain as he gazed at the darkened interiors of the Ladakh Fashion Arcade. A light burnt inside the shop.

Shadows indicated the presence of tourists, but the light wasn't strong enough for identification.

Aditya was late for dinner. Even if he quit the street and sprinted all the way to his hotel, he would not reach the Alpha Mess on time. Yet Aditya did not budge. Standing in the dark, he waited for the plump man to make his next move. Despite the man's odd behaviour, Aditya was still unsure of his intentions. But his suspicions were confirmed when barely a minute later, the man crossed the road and entered the Ladakh Fashion Arcade. The man had indeed been following him.

Aditya had no idea why he was being followed, but he could deal with that later. The pressing need was to get to the Alpha Mess as soon as possible. There was an intersection ahead down which a narrow road disappeared. The shadowed gully offered an easy exit for slipping away undetected.

The plump man was still searching for him inside the shop.

Aditya walked briskly. Turning at the intersection, he broke into a run. The noise of High Street fell behind. Aditya continued to run, halting only when he reached his hotel.

NIRVANA TRAVELS

The morning sun shone brightly through the windows of the dining hall at the Changspa Lodge, warming its cold stone floor. Every table was occupied, and cutlery clinked pleasantly against crockery in the cosy little room.

'We leave the day after tomorrow,' said a man with a scrappy beard, between mouthfuls of cornflakes. 'Do you know where the road to Khardung La starts?'

Aditya, seated opposite the man, nodded.

'Good. We leave from there at 12 p.m. sharp. You two should be at the road junction at least half an hour earlier. We need time to pack the luggage into the jeeps and get organized. Personally, I would have preferred to leave by 9 a.m., but I have a meeting scheduled for the morning, and, oh yes, Vikram—' the man paused, turning to the boy. 'Your father tells me you know Mr Reddy, the forest officer at Ranthambore. Is that right?'

'We both know him,' replied Vikram. 'Why?'

'He is arriving in Leh the day after tomorrow—a rushed trip I hear. I never understand why people travel all this distance and then return to Delhi the very next day.'

The bearded man shook his head. 'In any case, your dad has asked me to introduce Mr Reddy to the local range wardens and the police. It seems he has some leads on the tiger bone consignments being smuggled out of here to China, and he wants to follow up on them. If you are interested in meeting Mr Reddy, join me the day after tomorrow at 9 a.m.'

'We would love to meet him,' said Vikram eagerly. 'Right, Aditya?'

'Sure,' came the immediate response.

Mr Reddy's visit was an unexpected bonus. Mr Reddy* wasn't just a family acquaintance. He was a man the boys respected and admired for his bravery and dedication to his job.

'Well, don't be late. When I say 9 a.m., I mean 9 a.m. sharp. It's going to be a busy day for me, and I don't have a moment to spare.'

The bearded man fell silent, attacking the eggs on his plate.

Vikram's father had warned him about Dr Raghu Raman. 'Raghu is a brilliant field researcher,' he had told Vikram in Delhi. 'There's no better authority on snow leopards in this country. But he's a moody character—always in a hurry—and a man of few words. Don't get offended by him. He's a nice man at heart.'

Vikram guessed Dr Raghu Raman's age as around forty. His features were sunburnt and rugged. His beard

---

* Refer to *Ranthambore Adventure*.

and the mop of hair on his head were streaked with flecks of grey.

Dr Raman spoke next only when he was done and had poured himself a mug of coffee. 'See those mountains?' he said, pointing to the peaks across the valley. Clouds shrouded the slopes of the mountains Dr Raman indicated, but their snow-capped summits were visible. 'The tallest is called Stok Kangri and its summit is 20,000 feet above sea level. Our study area is on the far side of Stok Kangri, in the valleys behind. If you look carefully, you can see a glacier at the top of the mountain. One of our camps will be below that glacier.'

'Wow,' breathed Aditya. His eyes gleamed as he stared at Dr Raman.

'It will be cold up there, so make sure you carry enough woollies and a warm sleeping bag. The expedition will last two weeks, and I might as well warn you right now that this is a work trip, not a holiday. The gathering of scientific data involves hard, physical work. If it's a holiday you are looking for, forget it. The daily routine is tough, and I expect sincere effort. If either of you is not prepared to work or obey instructions, we can call the whole thing off right away.' Dr Raman's eyes glowered behind his coffee mug. Wooden-faced, he waited for a response to his ultimatum.

It was Vikram who replied. 'We'll do whatever you say, sir. You needn't worry about us.'

Neither of the boys expected Dr Raman's features to soften, but soften they did, and a smile creased his sunburnt countenance. 'Good. I'm glad. You won't regret it, I promise. I'll push you kids hard, but you'll enjoy yourselves. There will be others on the trip too. Volunteers from all over. We've been corresponding over the past few months, but I have never met them. Like you, their knowledge of the snow leopard is limited. It's my duty to teach them Himalayan ecology, and in return, they help me with my work.' Raghu dabbed his moustache with a napkin. 'I have to leave now, my students are waiting. We are headed for the Nubra Valley. I'll be spending the night in the valley and shall be back tomorrow evening. Both of you are joining me at 9 a.m. sharp the day after, is that right?'

'Yes, sir,' confirmed Vikram.

'No need to call me "sir", "Raghu" will do. Goodbye.' Setting his cap on his head, Raghu strode energetically to the door. A calm descended at the table in his wake, like the aftermath of a hurricane.

'Some character,' said Aditya, nibbling a toast.

'Dad says he has a reputation. He warned me about being booted out of the expedition if we don't perform. Better watch out, Aditya . . . No indiscipline.'

But Aditya wasn't listening. He was gazing at the peaks opposite. 'Camping under a glacier,' he murmured. 'This is going to be fun.'

There was no particular plan for the morning, and the boys lazed on the patio of their hotel. Vikram attempted reading a book, but his mind refused to comply. It wasn't long before he put the book down and concentrated on the thoughts buzzing in his head. Dwelling on the incidents of the past few days, he tried to analyze them. After thinking long and hard about this, he ruefully concluded he was getting nowhere. His thoughts kept running into blank walls, and all he succeeded in doing was throwing up questions without answers.

Meme Chacko alone could fit the pieces of the Tsering puzzle. Vikram decided it was pointless wasting time and energy over the problem, especially since they had received news that Meme Chacko was returning from the Changthang plateau later that evening. The hotel front desk had taken his call while they were dining with Reena and her parents. Meme Chacko had left a message saying he would meet them the next morning.

Confounding matters even more was the case of the man who had followed Aditya, a development that greatly troubled Vikram. Vikram was convinced that this spying incident could only be a result of their association with Tsering. But who could connect them with Tsering? Except for the Japanese birdwatcher and the kidnappers, no one had seen them with the Tibetan boy. The stalking seemed to point to an uncomfortable truth—that the Japanese man, or his friends the kidnappers, had arrived in Leh.

Vikram and Aditya had discussed the role of the Japanese man, concluding that he was involved with the Tsering kidnapping. It was his helpers who had joined forces with the kidnappers. Vikram had identified them and so had Nanju, the cook. Although the Japanese man had not taken part in the attack, it was clear he was involved. In fact, Vikram was convinced he was the mastermind behind the entire operation.

The tracking incident was sobering, but there was another way of viewing the matter; one that gave Vikram heart. Their being followed could only mean that Tsering was safe. The kidnappers were groping in the dark; they had no idea where the little boy was.

Their only engagement for the day was at 3 p.m., at the polo ground. A polo match was scheduled, and Aditya was keen to watch. Reena had promised to join them, and Dolma had indicated that she would try and make it too.

The boys had a late lunch at a traditional Ladakhi restaurant on High Street, feasting on momos and thukpa (a delicious stew of vegetables and meat). Later, they strolled to the polo ground.

The Leh polo ground is located on a flattened rise behind High Street. It has a small pavilion on one side and rows of stands on the other. A fair crowd had already assembled, and the boys spotted Reena waving to them from the upper section of the stands.

Although the origins of polo are obscure, it has been a popular sport in Himalayan areas like Ladakh for many hundreds of years. The game played in Ladakh is the original wild sport of the mountainous regions of Asia, different in many ways from the modern game played across the world.

Both Vikram and Aditya were taken aback by the furious pace of the game. Tiny Ladakhi ponies thudded across the ground at full speed, chasing a baseball-sized ball, which their riders swiped at with long sticks. There were goalposts at either end of the ground, and the aim was to smack the ball through the opposing team's goal. The three friends were enthralled by the game, and they joined the crowd in vociferously applauding the goals, which, unlike football, came fast and furiously.

Vendors did brisk business dishing out ice cream and snacks to the crowd. Aditya appreciated the dexterity of the riders, fascinated at the way they maintained their balance and controlled their mounts. It was a remarkable display of skill and control, and Aditya was quickly convinced that polo was a sport he wanted to learn.

People strolled along the edge of the ground, using it as a thoroughfare even while the match was in progress, the thunderous momentum of the galloping animals not bothering them at all. With practiced ease, they deftly slipped out of the way when the horses charged in their direction. Vikram couldn't help wincing when horses hurtled within inches of unconcerned pedestrians. It was during one of these hair-raising brushes that a plump man skipped out of the path of a group of speeding horses.

Aditya stiffened.

Instead of the blue shirt he had worn the previous day, the man was now wearing a green one. Yet his plump features were unmistakable, and Aditya recognized him as the man who had followed him.

Grabbing Vikram's arm, he pointed out the man.

'Do you think he has seen us?' asked Vikram.

A crowd of spectators was seated around them. Only if the man had closely examined the gathering would he have noticed them. 'I don't think so,' said Aditya, gazing at the plump figure walking unhurriedly to the old city.

Aditya rose to his feet.

Vikram reached up and grasped Aditya's arm, restraining him. 'Not you, Aditya. If anybody has to trail him, it has to be me. He knows you. It's safer that I follow him. You stay here, follow later.'

Vikram was thankful that Aditya did not argue. Instead, he urged Vikram to hurry. 'You better go quickly,' he said. 'Catch up with him before he reaches the exit. I'll join you later.'

Reena was so thoroughly absorbed in the game that she did not notice Vikram leave. Only after Vikram had woven his way through the crowd did Aditya put his hand on her shoulder. Aditya had to shout because the crowd suddenly roared, applauding a goal.

'Reena, please excuse us,' he said. 'Vikram and I have to go.'

Reena stared at him, not registering what he had said.

Aditya repeated his statement.

'Don't you want to wait for Dolma? She's coming here at four.'

'We'll be back by then. Vikram just remembered that we have to make a call. It's urgent. We'll take half an hour, max. Don't leave, wait for us.'

'You want to leave me here . . . . alone?'

'You could come with us,' offered Aditya.

Reena frowned at Aditya. It wasn't right that the boys abandon her. But Reena was a mild-mannered girl, and instead of protesting, all she did was issue a warning. 'Dolma and I will wait for you for half an hour. If you are not here by then, we shall leave.' She steadfastly refused to look at Aditya as he waved goodbye.

The upper section of the stands was packed, and Aditya had to pick his way through the crowd. He glanced at the gate on reaching ground level. The plump man had already quit the stadium, and Vikram was at the far exit. Aditya saw Vikram turn left at the gate. Keeping an eye on the galloping horses, Aditya walked quickly to the gate. Clouds were gathering in the skies. Stok Kangri and its neighbouring mountains were swathed in mist. Hurrying past tourists and peanut vendors, Aditya reached the exit and halted at the gate.

A dusty path wound down a hill slope, all the way to High Street. Aditya searched the path but found no sign of either Vikram or the plump man. He stood undecided. There was a distinct possibility that he would lose Vikram if he wandered cluelessly down the path. Vikram could have turned off into any of the side gullies. Reasoning that Vikram would eventually retrace his steps, Aditya decided to stay where he was.

A cold wind swept up from the Indus Valley, prompting Aditya to don his jacket. The old city of Leh lay spread before him. Prayer flags fluttered over tightly packed houses. Crows hovered above a rubbish dump. Above, Leh's abandoned palace reared sentinel-like from the slopes of the old city. The palace must have been an imposing structure in its heyday, but now it looked dilapidated. The royal family had relinquished it years ago, migrating to the city of Stok. Aditya had visited it on his previous trip, walking through its dark corridors and admiring the views from its imposing balconies. The palace was a popular tourist attraction, and even now a crowd was visible in its courtyard, squatting in a group, watching a performance. Some kind of cultural show thought Aditya distractedly as he glanced once more down the street. This time he saw Vikram waving from a gully below. Aditya walked quickly down to meet him.

'Your man walked down this street and entered a travel office round the bend ahead.'

'Travel office?' Aditya was taken aback.

Vikram shrugged. 'Maybe he works there. Should we check out the office?'

'Sure,' said Aditya, nodding.

Although the street was narrow—obviously a pedestrian street—scooters plied merrily along it. The thread-like street had a distinctly touristy feel, with shops, hotels and travel offices scattered along its length. The boys strolled casually, reading signboards and inspecting restaurants along the way.

'We're almost there,' said Vikram shortly. 'There's the travel office. Next to the phone booth.'

The phone booth was painted a bright, eye-catching yellow. The travel office was more restrained but equally striking with an imposing glass panel and a display of photographs of snow-covered mountains. The board above proclaimed 'Nirvana Travels'.

'Don't stop,' said Vikram. 'Walk past. Don't worry, the plump guy had no idea I was following him. No one's going to notice us.' After passing the office, he continued. 'Your plump man doesn't seem like a desk-job sort. His manner of dressing is too simple. Maybe he's a peon, the sort who runs errands for the office.'

'Could be,' consented Aditya. 'But a travel agency? What connection could they have with Tsering?'

They walked down the street, both lost in thought. A long-haired tourist pedalled past on a bicycle, cutting a path between a pair of scruffy dogs spread like carpets on the narrow lane. Three old Ladakhi ladies with wizened faces stared at the boys as they walked past.

Vikram halted. 'Aditya. You want to go river rafting on the Indus, don't you? Why don't we inquire about rafting at Nirvana Travels?'

It was a good excuse to enter the office, and Aditya was pleased with the idea. The boys turned and threaded their way back. Reaching the office of Nirvana Travels, Vikram entered, Aditya following.

THE JAPANESE MAN

The office was small, cosy and well-lit. Its walls were decorated with maps of Ladakh, a portrait of a snow leopard and other travel-related posters. Aditya spotted a picture of Tso Kar, identifying instantly its ring of mountains and the sediment of its white lake. At a table cluttered with brochures sat a pleasant-looking Ladakhi gentleman who smiled at the boys. There was a plywood cabin at one end of the room. The plump man stood beside its door. His head turned when Vikram and Aditya walked in.

The man behind the desk spoke: 'Please sit down, sirs. My name is Wangchuk, can I help you?'

'Why don't you tell us what you can offer,' suggested Aditya, seating himself.

'Oh! There are many things we can offer you.' Wangchuk gesticulated grandly. 'There are so, so many places to visit in Ladakh. We have beautiful Buddhist monasteries. One is there at Thikse, not very far from here. It is beautiful, but . . . I no think that you want monasteries.' Wangchuk's brow furrowed. 'You are outdoor boys, correct?'

'I outdoor boy . . . him—,' Aditya pointed at Vikram. '—him, indoor fellow. No monasteries please, only adventure.'

'Adventure!' Wangchuk inflated his chest, inhaling deeply. 'We can take you on treks, jeep safaris, cycling expeditions, river rafting . . . whatever you want. Ladakh has best lakes in the world: Pangong Tso, Tso Kar, Tso Moriri. I arrange everything for you. Tents, cooks, ponies, guides—we look after you well. We give you the best. If you don't want trekking, we give river rafting. We take you on the Indus or the Zanskar—'

Aditya listened with keen interest, but Vikram deliberately withdrew from the conversation, allowing his gaze to wander around the office. He saw the plump man open the cabin door and step inside. A glass panel rimmed the cabin and Vikram could see a fat, bespectacled man sitting behind the desk reading a newspaper. The plump man must have said something because the fat man suddenly straightened and stared in their direction.

Vikram pretended to pay attention to what Wangchuk was saying. '—for rafting we have half-day rides, or full day if you want. Maybe long expeditions for many days if you like. You tell us, we organize for you.'

'A single-day expedition is enough,' said Vikram. 'I don't want to camp out any more.'

'I told you, didn't I?' said Aditya. 'No adventure in this fellow. Have you got maps, Mr Wangchuk?'

Wangchuk cheerfully dug out a large map and spread it on the table.

Vikram heard the door to the travel office open. Floorboards creaked as somebody walked past. Vikram glanced disinterestedly at the visitor. The recognition was instantaneous. Though Vikram only managed a fleeting side view of the man, he was certain of his identity. It was the bogus Japanese birdwatcher. The man strode towards the plywood cabin without sparing a glance at the boys. The fat man's gaze was directed at the boys, and Vikram hoped his expression hadn't betrayed any sign of recognition.

'This is the Indus River,' Wangchuk traced it on the map with a pencil. 'We can start here, here or here.'

'I like gentle rapids,' said Vikram. 'I don't want to get wet.'

Wangchuk put down his pencil and stared at Vikram. 'You not want to get wet, sir?' Aditya held back a giggle. 'I suggest you not go rafting, sir. Everybody gets wet in rafting. Maybe you want to go to monasteries.'

'No, no!' exclaimed Aditya. 'Don't listen to him, of course we will get wet. Leave this to me, Vikram.'

Vikram feigned annoyance and looked away towards the cabin. There was no sign of the Japanese man.

Vikram blinked. How could it be? The man had been standing there just an instant earlier. The fat man was busy with his newspaper again, the plump man was missing too. Through the glass panel, Vikram spotted a door behind the fat man. Had the Japanese man vanished through the door? The bogus birdwatcher was their only link to the attempted kidnapping at Tso Kar. Vikram rose instinctively to his feet. Aditya and Wangchuk took no notice of him.

Striding to the cabin door, Vikram opened it and entered. The fat man jumped in his seat, looking up with a startled expression. Before the man could speak, Vikram shouted 'toilet!' and opened the door behind him. Vikram swept past the fat man, entering a dark corridor.

'No toilet here!' shouted the man agitatedly.

The corridor was short. At its far end, there was another door, which Vikram pushed open. There was a sudden glare of light. Vikram blinked. He was standing in a narrow lane between two buildings. Skipping over an open gutter, Vikram turned. The fat man's voluminous frame now filled the corridor. 'Toilet, very bad!' he said urgently and hurried away.

The Japanese man could have turned either left or right. Vikram chose left. Flies buzzed in the still air as he ran past a butcher's shop with chunks of meat dangling from hooks. There was the sound of traffic ahead and, through the slit-like mouth of the lane, he saw a bus drive past. Thoroughly disoriented, he stepped on to a wide intersection. It was when he saw the large minarets of the mosque at the head of the road that he got his bearings. He was standing on High Street.

A man at a shop door stepped forward, smiling. 'Sir, please come into my shop. Only look . . . No need to buy.'

Vikram shook his head, gazing at the road. The sky was overcast, and a cold wind blew, yet the street hummed with activity. Warm clothing had been donned for the day, and Vikram's eyes scanned a sea of colourful sweaters and jackets. There was no sign of either the Japanese man or his plump accomplice.

Vikram darted back down the lane, past the butcher's shop, to its opposite end. Here, the lane intersected the narrow street they had been walking along earlier. School had closed for the day and the passage was filled with a happy bunch of girls dressed in red sweaters. There was no trace of the Japanese man. The entrance to Nirvana Travels was a short distance ahead, and conceding defeat, Vikram walked towards it. Inside, he smiled at the fat man who was seated once again at his desk. The man grimaced and buried his head in his newspaper.

'There you are, Vikram,' greeted Aditya. 'Wangchuk here has been extremely helpful. We have decided on a full-day rafting trip. I've explained to him that we have to check with our friends before we can commit a date. He has given me his card, and we can call him once we are sure.'

Wangchuk beamed at Vikram.

'Thank you, Mr Wangchuk,' said Aditya, rising to his feet. They shook hands effusively, and Aditya patted Wangchuk on the back.

Vikram could see that the fat man was observing them keenly, though he was pretending otherwise. Vikram shook hands with Wangchuk and they stepped on to the street.

'Polo ground?' inquired Aditya.

Vikram nodded. 'Yes. The girls are waiting for us.'

'Hmm . . .' murmured Aditya appreciatively as they wove their way through a throng of schoolgirls. 'These Ladakhi girls are good-looking.'

'And what about Dolma?' queried Vikram innocently.

'Terrible temper.' Aditya changed the subject. 'Why on earth did you suddenly barge out of the office?'

'Didn't you see the Japanese birdwatcher?'

'No, and in any case, how would I have recognized him? I've never seen him.'

'Sorry, my mistake,' apologized Vikram, recollecting that Aditya had been up in the mountains with Tsering when the Japanese man had arrived. He explained the sequence of events to Aditya.

Aditya chuckled. 'So that's why the fat man was in a temper. You should have seen him after you left.' Aditya laughed. 'Remember the phrase "quiver with rage"? The fat man's belly really quivered—like a tub of jelly. It was a sight to behold.'

'We have a lead now,' said Vikram as they climbed the slope to the polo ground. 'The fact that the Japanese birdwatcher entered so authoritatively and then slunk out from the back proves that he knows the fat man well. Nirvana Travels is connected with the attempts on Tsering.'

'True,' agreed Aditya. 'Also, the guy who followed me works there. It all seems to point to Nirvana Travels . . . but not Wangchuk. I don't believe he is one of them. He just works there.'

They walked in silence for a while.

'Have you noticed anyone following us today?' asked Vikram.

'No, I haven't. I've been looking, but I haven't noticed anything odd. Why do you ask?'

'Well, think about it this way, Aditya. Ask yourself why they were following us. Why would anyone want to? After all, we are just another pair of Indian tourists—no big deal. The man who followed you yesterday did so because somebody asked him to. That somebody is definitely the fat man who owns Nirvana Travels. Their following us is a danger signal, which indicates how serious they are about getting Tsering. But it is also a good sign because it means that they have no clue where Tsering is. But the thing is that no one's following us now. That's unfortunate, and it has me worried.'

'*Unfortunate!*' Aditya looked at Vikram as if he was nuts.

'Don't you see that their following us confirms that they have no idea where Tsering is? Nobody tracking us worries me. They might have found him—'

Aditya came to a halt. 'Vikram! Will you stop worrying about Tsering? What is the point? Do *you* know where he is? For that matter, do you know *who* he is? Even if suspicious incidents take place, is there anything we can do? Do we have anybody to talk to? Anyone to share our fears and worries with? Do we?'

Vikram did not reply.

'Shall we just be happy that nobody's following us? Raghu's snow leopard trip is not going to be easy. He told us so. It's going to be hard. We have only this evening and tomorrow in Leh. Can we try and enjoy ourselves before leaving? Tomorrow, when Meme Chacko meets us, we'll tell him all we know. Then let's forget about this whole affair!'

Vikram did not entirely agree with Aditya, yet he had to admit that worrying served no purpose. Aditya was right—he might as well enjoy Leh.

Dolma and Reena were waiting at the entrance to the polo ground. The match had ended a few minutes earlier. Vikram was grateful that sparks did not fly between Dolma and Aditya. Both were polite to one another and refrained from exchanging derogatory remarks.

The teenagers visited the old palace. Later, despite near-freezing conditions, they climbed to the stupa above the palace. Prayer flags whipped back and forth in the wind as they huddled together, taking in the view of the Indus Valley and the city below. Green fields in the bowl of the valley traced the winding course of the Indus. The city of Stok was visible on the lower slopes of Stok Kangri. Gazing up the mountain, Vikram was glad they weren't camped beside the glacier atop Stok Kangri. A prominent white trail leaked from the packed clouds above the glacier. Vikram was in no doubt that the curtain of white was snow falling on the upper slopes of the mountain.

Later, they strolled the streets of the city and dined at a Ladakhi restaurant Dolma recommended. Though Vikram often gazed searchingly behind them during the evening, he failed to spot anybody following them.

TSERING'S STORY

Meme Chacko arrived in Leh well after midnight. Exhausted after a long, gruelling journey, he called the boys, postponing their meeting to 4 p.m.

They gathered at the designated time on the patio of the Changspa Lodge. Meme Chacko was dressed casually in jeans and a jacket. A grey beard covered the lower part of his face and his white hair was neatly brushed back. The lively sparkle in his eyes belied his age of seventy years.

'The far side of Stok Kangri,' he pondered after learning about the boys' plans. 'That's the area they call the Hemis National Park. I don't visit the region, so I'm not familiar with it. But I do know Raghu, and I have to warn you that he is not an easy person to get along with. My advice is to listen to him, obey his instructions and you will have a good time.'

Vikram nodded. 'Dad says exactly the same thing about Raghu—do what he says, and all will be fine. That's the mantra. We intend to follow it and have a great time.'

'You will,' said Meme Chacko. 'The Hemis National Park is a great wilderness. I wish I had the time to go with you, but there's so much going on.' Meme Chacko paused, his expression sobering. 'Now tell me everything that's happened since you arrived. Don't leave out anything.'

Meme Chacko listened attentively while Vikram enlightened him about the events in Leh.

'It's true,' agreed Meme Chacko when Vikram was done. 'You are being followed because of your connection with Tsering. I am deeply sorry to have dragged you into this mess. Your Tso Kar trip was ruined, and now you are being harassed in Leh.'

'Nobody has troubled us here,' said Vikram. 'We are enjoying Leh, and it isn't right to say our Tso Kar trip was ruined either. We had a super time there, and Tsering is a wonderful boy. Aditya and I like him a lot; helping him was only natural.'

Aditya waved a hand. 'It was no big deal, Meme Chacko. We didn't break any bones or get hurt. But one thing did trouble us, sir, and that was our complete ignorance. Place yourself in our situation, sir. We didn't know whom we were running away from or why we were being chased. It was crazy!' Aditya made a face. 'The thing is that the situation persists. We are still being chased and we still have no idea what the fuss is all about.'

Meme Chacko was quiet for a while. Then he laughed. 'How you boys pestered me at Tso Kar! Question after question. Endless queries. The irony of it all was that I had no answers. It might surprise you, Aditya, to know that I was as confused as you are. I was shocked by what happened at Tso Kar—kidnapping, guns, fist fights—I believe my ears when Nanju told me. At that time, even if I had wanted to, I couldn't have answered your questions.'

Meme Chacko rocked his chair, gazing unseeingly at the mountains. The sky was blue. Snow-capped peaks sparkled in the sunshine. 'My only connection to the school at Sumdo is the headmaster, who is a dear friend of mine. We've known each other for years. He always looks after me when I travel to that part of Ladakh. He's usually a happy, cheerful sort, always laughing and plenty of fun. But on this visit I found him disturbed—deeply so. He was scared, I could see that. He seemed terribly worried. It was while you were being shown around the school that he told me he had a problem, a situation he had no idea how to handle. As a friend, I offered to help him in any way I could. At first, he said there was nothing I could do for him, then he was silent. Soon after, he asked whether I would mind taking a little boy along with me to Tso Kar. It was a strange request, but not hard to fulfil, so I said yes. He insisted that we leave at once, and when we drove away with Tsering, I had no idea who he was. I was simply doing a favour for an old friend of mine. All I was told was that Tsering was somebody special and that I was to take good care of him. Later, when I stopped by the school after your escape from Tso Kar, the headmaster did explain things. He told me about Tsering. But there is a catch. Before telling me anything, he made me promise not to speak to anybody about it. He was emphatic that whatever he said was for my ears only.'

Meme Chacko paused. Then he laughed. 'There's no need to look so disappointed. The headmaster has allowed an exception in your case. You can thank Tsering for that. Apparently, he is very fond of you. He overruled the headmaster, insisting that you both be told the truth. So I can share this information with you.'

It was a warm summer afternoon. Bees flitted busily around the flowers, and in the distance, snow and mountains loomed ahead. But the grandeur of the peaks and the restfulness of the garden were lost on the boys. They listened to Meme Chacko with rapt attention.

'Everyone says the correct place to start a story is at the beginning. That's what I should do. But this story isn't your regular story. It's a strange one that has no beginning and no end. So if what I say appears to have no relevance to Tsering's story, please bear with me. We'll get there eventually.'

There was a long pause. Then Meme Chacko continued: 'Tsering's story, in a sense, is the story of Tibet. You might have read about Tibet in your geography books. It is the land that lies beyond the Himalayas, the great plateau that borders the Himalayan regions of India, Nepal and Bhutan. Geography books also call Tibet the "roof of the world", which is true. With an average height of 15,000 feet above sea level, the Tibetan plateau—or the Changthang as it is often called—lies high above the rest of the world. The winters there are severely cold and rainfall is limited. Although they call Tibet a plateau, it isn't particularly flat. Tibet is an immense, rolling stretch of land, intersected by mountain ranges, very much like what you saw at Tso Kar. In fact, the lakes of Tso Kar and Tso Moriri fall within the great Changthang, lying at its very edge.

'The people of Tibet have been Buddhists for centuries. Buddhism here in Ladakh came from Tibet. The monasteries, the monks, the way of life you see here were all imbibed from Tibet. Tibet and Ladakh might belong to separate countries today, but their people are still closely linked through religion. In both places, religion is extremely important, and it plays a central role in the lives of the people.

'A tradition of Buddhism practised here is to send one male child from every family to the local monastery to lead the life of a monk. The orange-robed monks that you see roaming the streets of Leh have all been entrusted to monasteries since childhood. They spend their lives in prayer and learning. Some of them later become lamas or head priests. The supreme leader, the spiritual head of all Tibetan lamas, is the Dalai Lama. You have heard of him, haven't you?'

The boys nodded.

'Maybe I should tell you the story of the Dalai Lama first. You will understand Tsering's story better if I do. The present Dalai Lama is the fourteenth in his line. The supremacy of the Dalai Lama was established in the fourteenth century, and he has been ruling Tibet since then. Even today, in spite of the Chinese takeover of his country, the people of Tibet still consider him to be their leader. That's quite something, isn't it? I don't know of many royal families that can boast about ruling their countries for that long. So, for all these centuries, it has been the Dalai Lama for Tibet. And it has always been the case that when the Dalai Lama grows old and passes on, the new Dalai Lama succeeds the previous one. That's the way it is, the traditional way. But the succession process for the Dalai Lama is not the same as it is for the royal families of the world. Generally, when the king of a country dies, his heir takes over. His successor is always chosen from his family. But that is not how it works for the Dalai Lama. For the Dalai Lama, and for Tibet, the method of succession is different—fascinatingly different.

'The Dalai Lama is a religious head. They say that soon after he dies, he is reborn. It is believed that his spirit . . . his consciousness, does not die. It passes on into a fresh body, and the Dalai Lama is born again. I know this sounds difficult to believe, but for Tibetans, this is true. The Dalai Lama is reborn on earth and not necessarily into a royal family. It might seem odd, but in most cases, he is born to a simple peasant family. Now here's the interesting part. Nobody knows where the Dalai Lama has been born. The new Dalai Lama has to be found. But how do you identify an infant, a child who can't walk or talk, as the next Dalai Lama? The search and the Dalai Lama's discovery is a divine process, a process understood only by holy monks, and the task is left entirely in their hands.

'Whenever a Dalai Lama dies, a senior group of monks begin their search. The monks put the word out inquiring for special signs that may have occurred during the birth of children. They visit a lake known for its prophetic vision. Through dreams, divine portents, visions and observation of uncommon events, the monks are finally led to a home where the Dalai Lama could have been born. After requesting permission of the parents, the monks "interview" the selected child. This part is difficult, considering that the child is a baby who cannot talk.

'The monks conduct a number of simple yet meaningful tests, chief amongst them being the identification of articles that belonged to the child in his previous life. Things like the Dalai Lama's shoes, his prayer beads, his prayer wheel. These possessions of the Dalai Lama are placed in front of the child along with exact replicas. So there will be two pairs of shoes, two sets of prayer beads, two sets of prayer wheels, and so on and so forth. From these items, the child has to choose those that belonged to him in his previous life. If the child is indeed the Dalai Lama, he will pick those objects that belonged to him. If the child cannot select the right articles, then he obviously isn't the reincarnated Dalai Lama, and the monks move on to the next house. The monks keep searching till they find the boy who selects all articles correctly. And when such a boy is found, he is proclaimed the new Dalai Lama.

'Just think about it, boys. Over the centuries, the Dalai Lama has been born again and again. Tensing Gyatso, the current Dalai Lama, was born in a modest village to a simple family. The monks were led to his home, and after testing him, they proclaimed him as the Dalai Lama. Tensing

Gyatso is the same person that was the first Dalai Lama back in the fourteenth century.'

The boys sat in rapt silence.

Meme Chacko leaned forward. 'You might ask how all this is connected to Tsering? I can see the question hovering on your lips.' Meme Chacko smiled and paused for effect. 'Your little friend Tsering, like the Dalai Lama, is a reborn lama.'

Vikram and Aditya were dumbstruck. Vikram couldn't believe his ears. Aditya's mouth popped open.

'Tsering,' continued Meme Chacko, 'was a very famous lama in his previous life. He died some time ago of old age somewhere in Tibet. Soon after he died, monks began the search for him. One particularly holy man was told in a dream that the late lama had been reborn in a certain village in central Tibet. The monk also had a vision that the house in which the lama had been born stood beside a large lake. The village that the holy man had seen was Tsering's village, and there were five houses there that stood near the shores of a large lake. Tsering's home was one of those houses. Tsering was a little baby, barely a year old, when the monks came searching for him. As in the case of the Dalai Lama, they tested his ability to identify the possessions of his previous life from amidst other similar objects. In each and every case, Tsering selected the correct object. The news soon spread that the dear departed lama had been found again . . . and yes, little Tsering is that famous lama.'

There was a long-drawn silence.

'I can't believe it,' whispered Aditya, breaking the silence.

Vikram too finally found his tongue. 'But,' he said, 'if Tsering is a famous lama, why are people chasing him? Why do they want to kidnap him?'

Meme Chacko sighed. 'Yes, that's the next question: why are people chasing him? To answer that, Vikram, I will have to explain a little Tibetan history to you. The Tibet of today is a troubled place. The Dalai Lama is the supreme leader of Tibet, yet he doesn't live there any more. He now lives in India. As I said earlier, for all these past centuries, it was the Dalai Lama who ruled Tibet. Under his rule, the country was peaceful and people prospered. But in 1958, the Chinese occupied Tibet, and the Dalai Lama was forced to flee. The present Dalai Lama was a young man when he fled through the mountain passes into India. Since that fateful year, the Dalai Lama has never returned to Tibet. Instead he has lived in exile in India, at Dharamshala in Himachal Pradesh. Many thousands of his countrymen came with him to India. Over the years, refugees from Tibet, seeking a safe haven, have flooded into our country—and all have found a home here.

'The Dalai Lama is now a leader in exile. Modern Tibet is ruled by the Chinese. The people there are divided. Though the majority of today's Tibetans love and respect the Dalai Lama, there are those whose loyalty is to the Chinese government.

'As I mentioned earlier, about ten years ago, a very famous lama died, and when the Dalai Lama's followers searched for his reincarnation, they selected Tsering when he passed their tests. They proclaimed him as the new lama. But the Chinese government disagreed. They refused to accept Tsering as the new lama. Instead, they appointed their own monks who, through a different process—an entirely non-religious one—selected another boy whom they proclaimed as the next lama. This was a peculiar situation; obviously the lama who had died could not have been reborn in two separate bodies. One of the two boys was the true reincarnation, the other wasn't.

'The government loudly proclaimed that it had found the reincarnation of the dear departed lama, and it celebrated in grand style. But a rumour quickly spread that this boy wasn't the correct one and that the Dalai Lama did not believe he was the new lama. People whispered that the Dalai Lama's monks had found another boy who they said was the real lama. Though the Dalai Lama has been in exile for more than fifty years, the people of Tibet still believe in his word. And soon, despite the government proclamation, it was Tsering whom the people accepted as the real lama.

'This dispute took place several years ago, when Tsering was still an infant. It went on till one day, Tsering—barely two years old then—suddenly vanished. Nobody knew where he had gone or who had taken him. The kidnappers cleverly covered their trail, leaving no clues whatsoever. Tsering's disappearance suited the government and their chosen lama. With Tsering out of the way, their boy no longer had any competition. They announced that the controversy was over, and their chosen youngster was now the undisputed lama.

'Though the years passed without any news of young Tsering, his memory remained in the hearts of the people. Not believing he was dead, the monks launched a search for him. It was a secret operation that no one knew of. The search was eventually successful, and Tsering was discovered a month ago in a remote Tibetan village not far from the Ladakh border. The details of how Tsering was located and of his rescue are still a secret. It was a hush-hush affair; even the Dalai Lama's people at Dharamshala had no idea that the boy had been found and freed from captivity. Tsering was then smuggled into India by a nomadic Changpa family. Tibetan nomads from across the border handed Tsering to Indian nomads.

'Although we found Tsering at Sumdo, but that was never the plan. In fact, Tsering's rescuers had never intended to halt at Sumdo. The original plan had been to smuggle him into Leh and then on to Dharamshala where he would be handed over to the Dalai Lama. But his rescuers ran into trouble after crossing the border. Their safe entry into India had lulled them into a false sense of security. They had underestimated the determination of Tsering's kidnappers, and that turned out to be a terrible mistake. During a victory celebration, his pursuers struck. They were in rugged, high mountain territory at the time. It was a remote and uninhabited area. Heavily outnumbered and outgunned, Tsering's liberators fought a losing battle. When it became obvious they would lose, one of Tsering's liberators stole away from the conflict, taking the boy with him. After a long, eventful flight through the mountains, they took shelter at the school at Sumdo.

'Tsering's arrival in Sumdo was like a bolt from the blue. Like all Tibetans, the headmaster was aware of the controversy surrounding the young lamas. Tsering's disappearance had saddened him, and as time passed, he had lost hope for the unfortunate boy. You can imagine his surprise when one fine day the little lama was delivered at his doorstep.

'But his joy at the reappearance of Tsering was short-lived. Sumdo, as you have seen, is a tiny village. Outsiders are immediately noticed. At about the time we arrived, strange men were seen in Sumdo, asking questions about the school. The headmaster is a simple scholarly soul. He is an excellent administrator, perfectly suited for his job, but the matter of Tsering was beyond his capacity. This matter was no ordinary one. It had to do with kidnapping, violence and international intrigue—something he could not handle. Our appearance in his time of need was like a godsend to him. When you look back on it, sending Tsering with us was a shrewd move. At that time, the kidnappers were sure he was being sheltered at the school. His disappearance baffled them. But as you know that happy state of affairs did not last long. The events from then on are better known to you than me.'

Vikram stared at the ground, his mind in a whirl. He had suspected all along that Tsering was an important boy. Yet he had been thoroughly unprepared for Meme Chacko's revelation. Tsering . . . a lama . . . a man who was reborn! How was he to believe such a story? He had never heard of such things before.

Meme Chacko cleared his throat. 'I have been asked to swear both of you to silence. Remember, that was the pledge you gave me. And I repeat once more, the story of Tsering is only for your ears.'

'Why?' asked Aditya.

'Several reasons, Aditya. But most importantly because this is an internal dispute amongst Tibetans. They do not want to turn it into an international incident. A cross-border conflict like this can cause unnecessary tension. Neither of the warring parties wants government interference. The relationship between the two countries is already delicate. India and China have a basketful of unsolvable problems; they do not want to add the story of Tsering to this.'

'But who are these people chasing Tsering?' asked Aditya. 'Who attacked us at Tso Kar?'

Meme Chacko shrugged. 'No one knows for sure. Most are Tibetans from across the border. But the headmaster suspects that they are being helped from this side of the border too. Then there is this Japanese man. Your conclusion that he is the ringleader might be correct. It's a clever ruse . . . a Japanese man controlling the Indian operation. Hundreds of Japanese visit Ladakh every year. He could easily pass off as a harmless tourist. Your discovery of his connection with Nirvana Travels could be an important lead. Tsering's friends here will surely follow up on it.'

Meme Chacko looked at his watch. 'You boys certainly ask a lot of questions. The jeep I had asked for must have arrived by now. I have made—'

Vikram interrupted the elderly gentleman mid-sentence. 'Are we going to meet Tsering?' he asked eagerly.

Meme Chacko looked at Vikram in exasperation. 'Will you let me finish? Yes, I have made arrangements for a meeting with Tsering. But don't get your hopes up. The meeting might not work out. We have to contend with Tsering's enemies. You know the reality. We will have to drop the idea if we feel we are being tailed. Keep that in mind. Now, when I was interrupted by Vikram, I was saying that the jeep that was to take us has probably arrived. I'll check. In the meantime, I suggest you get ready to leave. Don't forget your warm clothes. It will turn chilly in the evening.'

PHYANG

An army Jonga was waiting at the hotel gate.

Vikram laced his boots and collected his jacket. In five minutes, they were seated in the Jonga—Meme Chacko in front, the boys at the back.

Vikram felt a lightness inside. He was thrilled at the prospect of meeting Tsering again. But his eagerness was held in check, sobered by Meme Chacko's warning that someone could be following them. Everyone kept a sharp lookout. Vikram and Aditya surveyed the road behind while Meme Chacko probed the area on either side of the road. Exiting Leh, their Jonga turned on to the Srinagar highway. A milestone flashed past informing them that Srinagar lay 420 kilometres ahead. Shadows crept across the Indus Valley as the sun dipped westward. It was warm, and the boys enjoyed the feel of the wind on their faces.

Leh quickly fell behind. With no homes or trees to block the view, their field of vision increased. They could see for miles on end. There was nobody following them; the road was empty.

'Surprising,' murmured Meme Chacko. 'I thought there would be a problem, but no one is following us. So much for my elaborate plans. There's an army depot ahead where I've arranged for a change of vehicles. The plan is to drive into the depot, change vehicles inside and exit from a hidden back gate in a civilian van. The commanding officer of the depot is a friend, and he extended permission to park our van inside. Not only that, but he granted me another favour. There's a checkpost at the depot, and he has promised to bring the barrier down for ten minutes. The barrier will effectively block the highway for that period. That should give us enough time to get ahead and lose anyone trying to follow us.'

'Wow!' said Aditya. 'Now that's what I call a plan. The whole road blocked off!'

The planning was scrupulous and thorough, thought Vikram. And rightly so, every possible precaution had to be taken for Tsering.

After a while, they passed a checkpost and the Jonga pulled off the road, entering a fenced compound through an arched gate. There was a van waiting for them as Meme Chacko had promised. It was a small Maruti Omni with Ladakhi number plates. The changeover was quick. They jumped out of the Jonga and climbed into the van. The driver, a smiling Ladakhi gentleman with dark hair and a thin moustache, exited the compound through a back gate. They travelled down a small, dusty track for a couple of kilometres and then rejoined the main road.

There were no cars on the road.

Meme Chacko was pleased with himself. 'The plan's working,' he smiled. 'The checkpost barrier is down. If all goes well, we should reach our destination soon.' Gesturing at the driver, he said, 'This is my friend, Dawa. The van is his, and he has been kind enough to drive us around for the evening.'

The boys smiled at Dawa who grinned and nodded.

A short distance ahead, they slowed and turned off the main road on to a smaller one that led to the mountains. A jeep passed them at the intersection, turning left for Leh.

They drove along a broad sloping plain, mostly barren, except for a distant patch of green where a typical Ladakhi village nestled beside a snow-fed river. On one side of the village, a large red monastery rose imposingly on a hill.

'Phyang village,' informed Dawa.

Soon the barren slopes fell behind and they drove between rolling fields. Stands of wheat and barley, bright in the setting sun, rustled in a mild breeze. They passed an elderly Ladakhi lady in red robes, bent double under a load strapped to her forehead. Red-cheeked children played beside the road. Two pretty girls in traditional clothing waved as they passed by.

Although just twenty kilometres from Leh, it seemed they had travelled to a different world. There were no tourists, no bustle, no movie posters, no hotels and no western-dressed Ladakhi youth. Here at Phyang, Vikram felt he had stepped into a timeless place. Leh might have changed, but Phyang reflected another existence—the traditional one that had persisted for centuries.

A bumpy road wove between the fields. About halfway through the valley, Dawa halted the van under a stand of poplar trees. A toothless old man with thick spectacles sat by the roadside, perched on a fallen log. He smiled at them, turning a prayer wheel in his hand.

Dawa alighted from the vehicle, requesting the others to follow. They tramped behind Dawa, across a grassy slope sliced by several streams. Wagtails chased insects across the flashing trails of water. A hoopoe with a black crown pecked at the ground. One of the streams was fast-flowing and wide. They traversed it on a log bridge, crossing to a house with an orchard packed with apple trees. Dawa knocked on the door of the house.

Standing beneath the fruit-laden trees, Vikram wondered how he should greet Tsering. Should he hug him or bow reverently before him? When they had met Tsering last, he was just a scruffy kid with soulful eyes. But now they knew him as a revered lama, a reincarnated soul, a holy son of Tibet with a divine destiny.

While Vikram deliberated, a Ladakhi lady with plaited hair and an apron-like dress opened the door. Dawa obviously knew the lady well because a hearty conversation ensued with loud laughter and energetic waving of arms. Soon after, she called loudly, and two boys came running from a nearby field.

The boys spoke to the lady in Ladakhi. Dawa informed them that Tsering had been working in the fields with the boys. 'But the boys say that Tsering returned to the house sometime back,' went on Dawa. 'As he's not at home, the boys are going to look for him. Their mother and I will also search. Please wait here.'

Meme Chacko walked Vikram and Aditya around the house while they waited. 'This is where the cattle are kept,' he said, pointing to a door leading down to a basement. 'Often during winters, snow leopards break into such cattle pens. For some reason, the leopards kill all the cattle in the pen, and this obviously angers villagers. The villagers are compensated for their cattle, but they don't like it at all. To them, the snow leopard is a—' Meme Chacko halted in mid-sentence on hearing a shout.

It was Dawa, and there was an urgency to his call. They hurried to him, crossing the log bridge and the grassy slope. They found Dawa, the lady and the boys at the road, grouped around the old man with the prayer wheel.

Dawa's expression was tense. 'The old man says a car was parked here sometime ago. He says he saw a young boy being dragged through the fields and locked into the car.'

Vikram and Aditya looked at each other in shock. Meme Chacko turned still.

The lady with the plaited hair knelt before the old man. Staring at the thick lenses masking his eyes, she spoke to him with slow, measured words.

The man was silent for a while. When he finally spoke, his speech was slow and halting.

Dawa translated for the others. 'The car was parked in exactly the same spot as our car. The old man says he didn't pay it any attention. It was only when he heard scuffling sounds that he looked at the vehicle. He saw a boy with something wrapped around his face being pushed into it.'

The lady spoke to the old man again.

Dawa translated. 'He doesn't know what time they left. He says it was warmer than it is now. It was a car, maybe a jeep; he doesn't know.'

Vikram spoke up. 'Ask him if he remembers the colours. Was the vehicle white, green or red?'

Dawa spoke to the old man, but the lady shook her head, saying something.

'He is a very old man, according to the lady,' explained Dawa. 'It's surprising he's spoken so much. He doesn't know the difference between a car and a jeep, and he won't remember colours.'

Vikram tried again. 'Ask him when he saw the boy. The time is important. Could Tsering have been in the jeep that we saw at the highway junction?'

Dawa spoke to the lady who stooped once more before the old man.

'No,' said Dawa after a while. 'Time has no meaning for him. The answer he gave earlier, that it was warmer then, is the best we can get.'

Vikram felt sorry for the lady. Her face was a ghostly white. Tears had gathered in her eyes, and she was struggling to hold them back. Tsering's kidnapping had devastated her. The responsibility of looking after the little lama had been hers.

There wasn't much else to be said. Bidding an unhappy farewell to the lady and her children, they set off on their return journey to Leh.

Meme Chacko was deeply upset, and it showed on his face when he bid them goodbye at their hotel. 'This is the worst thing that could have happened. Vikram, you will have to give my apologies to Dr Raghu. I was to have joined you tomorrow at the forest department headquarters to meet Mr Reddy, but I won't be coming now. Dawa and I are going to do everything we can to find Tsering. You boys enjoy your holiday. I can feel your distress, but there is little you can do. Try and forget this happened. Have a good time, and I shall meet you when you return to Leh.'

Try and forget this happened, thought Vikram bitterly as he sat with Aditya in the tiny garden of their hotel. How on earth could they forget? Tsering was their friend! They had laughed and played with him. The little boy had found a place in their hearts, and after learning about his status, the young lama was even more special.

The sun had set, and the night was turning chilly. Aditya ordered a pot of mint tea and poured two cups.

Vikram warmed his hands around his cup. 'Do you think Tsering was in the jeep that passed us at Phyang junction?' he asked.

'Don't know,' replied Aditya. 'Difficult to say, but he could have been.'

'That's what I think too. It is possible. I can't remember a thing about the occupants, do you?'

Aditya shook his head. 'No, I wasn't looking. But I remember the jeep, particularly its green top. It's rare to see a hardtop Gypsy in these parts, that's why I remember it. If I saw it again, I'd recognize it.'

'If we see it again,' murmured Vikram, thinking. 'Leh is a small town. There can't be more than a hundred jeeps here.'

'Are you suggesting we start searching for jeeps?'

Vikram sighed. 'Forget about it. We should start packing for our trek instead. We don't have much time tomorrow, considering that we have to leave at 9 a.m. sharp with Raghu. I've made a list of things to carry. Let's see—' he paused, digging out a piece of paper from his wallet. '—toothpaste, toothbrush, hat, sunscreen lotion, binocs, water bottle, notebook, pen, socks, chappals—'

'Don't remind me!' groaned Aditya.

In a thoroughly subdued mood, the boys packed and readied their rucksacks for their trek. Every item had to be carefully thought of and packed. If they left something behind, they would have to make do without it. Raghu was taking them to a mountain wilderness where there were no shops and no roads.

It was late by the time the boys finished packing, and after a quick meal, they fell asleep.

Vikram and Aditya were at the breakfast table by 8 a.m. Clouds blanketed the Stok mountains, but there was a blue sky above. They sat at a table near the window, absorbing the warmth of the morning sun. Vikram hadn't slept well the night before, tossing and turning, thinking of Tsering.

Finally, only after a plan had crystallized in his head had he fallen asleep. He spoke to Aditya while they waited for their eggs.

'Aditya, we have to make an attempt to find Tsering. We can't abandon him and leave.'

Aditya stared at Vikram, not replying.

'I did some thinking last night,' continued Vikram. 'The Japanese man is the key, you know that. If anybody knows where Tsering is, it's him; he arranged the kidnapping.'

Aditya nodded in agreement.

'We know that there is a connection between the man and Nirvana Travels. So if he planned the kidnapping, the fat owner of Nirvana Travels is in this too. The fat man knows where Tsering is too.'

The eggs arrived at their table. There was a pause as both boys attacked the food on their plates.

Aditya finished first. Wiping his lips on the back of his sleeve, he spoke. 'So what you are saying is that we hang about Nirvana Travels and hope that the Japanese man appears. We don't have that kind of time, Vikram. Raghu will be here at 9 a.m. sharp.'

Vikram held up a hand. 'Listen to me. Let me tell you what I've been thinking. If the Japanese guy arranged the kidnapping, he would have had to first arrange for a vehicle, right? Some means of transport would be required to take Tsering to their hideout. If we assume that the hardtop Gypsy was the kidnap vehicle, then as per our thinking the Japanese man arranged that jeep. It is obvious that the Japanese man is not a resident of Leh. He doesn't have his own vehicle. So if he had to arrange one, who do you think he would have approached?'

'Nirvana Travels,' said Aditya unhesitatingly.

'Yes, Nirvana Travels! Maybe your friend Wangchuk the salesman did the booking.'

Aditya's eyes gleamed. 'It is possible.'

'You made good friends with Wangchuk, Aditya. If he booked any jeeps yesterday, do you think he might tell you?'

'I can talk to him,' said Aditya. 'I don't see any reason why he won't tell me.'

'It's a beginning,' said Vikram. 'If we find the jeep, we could get further clues from there.'

'Wait a second, I'll check Wangchuk's business card.' Aditya extracted the card from his wallet. 'Working hours 9 a.m. to 5 p.m., it says. Drat!'

Vikram looked at his watch. It was 8.30 a.m.

'Do you want to stay behind, Aditya?' suggested Vikram. 'You don't have to meet Mr Reddy. I have to. Mr Reddy is family to Dad and me.'

It was just the previous year that the boys had helped Mr Reddy nab a dreaded tiger poacher.* Aditya held Mr Reddy in high esteem and had been looking forward to meeting him. But at this moment, Tsering came first, and Aditya agreed with Vikram that he should stay behind.

Finishing their breakfast, the boys returned to their room and transferred their luggage to the hotel lobby.

---

* Read *Ranthambore Adventure*.

At 8.45 a.m., Aditya called Nirvana Travels, but there was no reply.

Raghu strode into the lobby exactly one minute after 9 a.m. Their rucksacks would have to be transferred to his jeep, he informed them. They wouldn't be returning to the hotel after the conference as there was no time. On learning that Aditya would not be accompanying them, he warned him that they would be leaving from the Khardung La junction at 12 p.m. sharp. If he did not show up by then, he would be left behind.

Aditya looked at his watch as Raghu departed with Vikram. Raghu, the stickler for time, had let himself down, he noted wryly. It was five minutes past 9 a.m. sharp.

DETECTIVE ADITYA

Aditya called Nirvana Travels a few minutes later. It was past 9 a.m., and the office should have opened. His call was answered by Wangchuk. Yes, of course he remembered Aditya, and no, he had not made any bookings for a jeep the day before. When Aditya quizzed him about a Japanese visitor, he told Aditya that several Japanese tourists visited Nirvana Travels every day and that yesterday none had asked for a jeep.

'Wangchuk,' said Aditya, thinking quickly. 'I need a jeep today. Can you recommend somebody who supplies reliable jeeps?'

'We always hire jeeps from Zeenat Automobiles. You can call them.' Wangchuk helpfully gave Aditya the telephone number.

'Where is Zeenat Automobiles?' asked Aditya.

'Right beside the airport, you can't miss it. It is a big open yard with lots of cars, jeeps and vans parked inside.'

Aditya thanked Wangchuk, promising to get back to him when he finalized the dates of their river rafting trip.

Aditya strode back and forth across the hotel patio deep in thought. Wangchuk had not booked a jeep yesterday. Could the fat boss of Nirvana Travels have asked for the vehicle? It was probable, thought Aditya. And if it was the fat man who had done the booking, he would have booked the vehicle through his reliable supplier, Zeenat Automobiles.

Aditya decided to visit Zeenat Automobiles. He would have to move fast though. He looked at his watch. Less than three hours remained till 12 p.m. sharp. Zeenat Automobiles was all the way down at the airport. Walking there would take too long. He needed transport.

Aditya called Meme Chacko's lodge but was informed that he had stepped out.

Reena's parents had a vehicle and a driver. He dialled her number, but the line was busy. Aditya hesitated. Then drawing a breath, he dialled Dolma.

Dolma answered.

'Hi Dolma, this is Aditya. Do you still have that jeep of yours?'

'Yes, I do,' came the guarded reply.

'I have to go somewhere urgently, a place called Zeenat Automobiles, near the airport. Can you take me there?'

There was a pause and then, 'Okay, I'll be there in five minutes.'

Dolma arrived in a white Gypsy with a soft-top. She wore black leather boots, jeans and a T-shirt. A denim jacket was slung over her shoulders. Exchanging greetings, they set off. Dolma was an impatient driver, and Aditya had to hold on to his seat as she drove headlong through the crowded streets, dodging pedestrians and animals.

'Why do you want to go to Zeenat Automobiles?' inquired Dolma, swerving to avoid a cow. Her long hair flowed behind her, and the morning sun gleamed on her long, dangling earrings.

Aditya had no intention of telling Dolma the truth. 'Raghu, the snow leopard man, needs jeeps to take us to the starting point of our trek today,' he replied.

Dolma wrinkled her brow. 'Isn't it a bit late for organizing transport? Vikram said that you are leaving at noon.'

'There's been a problem,' lied Aditya. 'Raghu's travel agent backed out this morning. And since Raghu is caught up with a visitor, he has asked me to make the arrangements.'

Dolma sped down a sloping road to the bowl of the valley. Soon the road flattened out, and a military fence ran endlessly on their left. Aditya spotted the airport's runway. Wangchuk's directions were perfect. Ahead was a board with Zeenat Automobiles printed on it. There was a fence with an open gate, which Dolma swung through.

They entered a dusty compound where several vehicles were parked. Aditya spotted the green hardtop Gypsy immediately, parked amidst a row of jeeps. His pulse quickened as he alighted; this had to be the same vehicle they had seen at the Phyang junction. Three men were working on the jeeps. Each had a bucket and was busy scrubbing a vehicle. Aditya walked towards the jeeps, as Dolma followed him.

'Why do you want a hardtop Gypsy?' asked Dolma when Aditya halted beside the green vehicle.

'I have one at home,' Aditya replied untruthfully. 'Its top is green too. Isn't that a coincidence?'

There was only one roofed building in the yard, which Aditya assumed was the office. A man with his hands in his pockets had stepped through its door and was walking towards them.

'Do people rent hardtop jeeps?' asked Aditya when the man halted beside them.

'Not often,' replied the man. 'Open jeeps are preferred.' He was dressed in distinctive Muslim robes and a straggly beard covered most of his face.

'Hardtop vehicles are useful in winter,' said Dolma. 'It's bitterly cold then and they are far more efficient than soft-tops for retaining heat. Don't take a hardtop, Aditya. I'm sure Raghu will prefer a soft-top jeep.'

'Did you hire out this vehicle yesterday?' asked Aditya, casually running his hands along the dusty fibreglass hood.

'I think so, yes—' The man broke off, speaking in Ladakhi to one of the men cleaning the jeeps.

The cleaner thought for a while then shouted something back.

'Yes, it was rented out yesterday,' said the man with the straggly beard. He introduced himself as Mr Iqbal, adding that he was the manager.

Aditya discussed rental rates with him. When Aditya told Iqbal that he didn't require the vehicles today, but possibly the next day, he saw Dolma staring at him.

Ignoring Dolma's incredulous gaze, Aditya continued to talk to Iqbal, stating that he and his friends were planning a camping trip to Pangong Tso. Was Iqbal sure that the vehicles were readily available?

Iqbal confirmed the availability of his jeeps.

Aditya haggled with the bearded manager. Dolma pitched in and lowered the price substantially more than Aditya could have.

'May I have your business card?' requested Aditya when the negotiations were over. 'I will confirm tomorrow.'

Aditya thanked Iqbal for the card. Then, as an afterthought, he went on. 'There is one more thing, Mr Iqbal. Can you tell me how I can locate the gentleman who drove this green jeep yesterday?' Iqbal stared inquiringly at him and Aditya continued. 'I know this is a strange request, but the man who was driving it yesterday behaved very rudely. My friend Vikram and I were strolling near the market last evening when this vehicle came shooting round the corner at the Moravian Church. The jeep knocked my friend down. The driver refused to stop, instead he waved a fist at us and drove away. I remember his vehicle because it had a hardtop. I am sure it is this same jeep, and I would be grateful if you could help me because people who drive so dangerously are a menace. Something has to be done about them.'

'Don't worry,' added Aditya when he saw Iqbal hesitate, 'I promise not to go to the police. This is a private matter.'

Aditya winked at Dolma while Iqbal consulted the cleaner.

The Ladakhi girl returned a glacial gaze.

'Arif here delivered the jeep,' said Iqbal. 'He remembers that he drove it to Hotel Leh Palace and handed the keys to a Japanese gentleman. I remember now—this booking was done through Nirvana Travels yesterday morning. They wanted a hardtop Gypsy, and if I recollect correctly, the keys were to be delivered to room twenty-nine.' Iqbal smiled at Aditya. 'I hope that will help you.'

'Thank you so much, sir,' replied Aditya warmly. 'My friend and I will speak to the Japanese gentleman. He should be warned not to drive rashly.'

They walked back to Dolma's jeep. Aditya thanked Mr Iqbal again and waved goodbye as Dolma pulled on to the main road.

'Hotel Leh Palace, I presume?' inquired Dolma, turning for the city.

'How did you guess?' grinned Aditya.

Dolma spoke in a breezy tone. 'I have heard a lot of lies this morning. The first was about Raghu requiring jeeps immediately. Then there was another about a trip to Pangong Tso. You reserved the best for the last, didn't you, about Vikram being knocked over?'

'Seriously,' said Aditya in as earnest a tone as he could manage. 'The reason Vikram didn't come with me this morning is because he had to go to the doctor. We don't know whether his knee will stand up to a two-week trek.'

Dolma stepped on the brakes, forcing the car to a screeching halt. Then she erupted, tempest-like. 'Don't lie to me, Aditya!' she shouted, her eyes flashing in anger.

Aditya darted a backward glance, half expecting a vehicle to smash into them from behind. Luckily, the road was empty.

Dolma's cheeks had turned crimson, and her chest was heaving. 'There is a limit to the nonsense I can take from you. If you think you can take me for granted, you might as well get off here. *Right now!*'

Dolma glared at Aditya, her delicate jaw set at a stubborn angle. It was clear to Aditya that he had crossed a limit. He would have to tell Dolma the truth or get off, as she demanded. Although Aditya had promised Meme Chacko not to speak of Tsering to anyone, he had no choice with Dolma. Her cooperation was vital. Tsering's freedom could depend upon it. Aditya decided to speak, but before doing so, he insisted on a pledge of secrecy from Dolma, to which the girl grudgingly agreed.

Dolma parked the jeep beside a gurgling stream of water. A cold breeze rustled the leaves of the poplar trees lining the road as Aditya sketchily outlined Tsering's kidnapping.

'Don't press me for details,' pleaded Aditya when he concluded. 'We have barely two hours to find Tsering. Can we move on immediately?'

Dolma was silent during the short drive to the hotel.

Hotel Leh Palace was an imposing double-storeyed building situated on the lower slopes of the city. Dolma halted in its shaded parking lot.

'Now what?' asked Dolma, cutting the engine.

'We have to find the occupant of room twenty-nine,' said Aditya.

'Yes, Aditya, we can find the man. And then?'

'I don't know, Dolma,' Aditya replied honestly. 'What can I say at this stage? Let's find the man first. We can worry about the next step later. I'm going to try and get the keys to room twenty-nine. The plan is simple. I'll try and bluff my way through—ask the desk manager for the keys, pretending I'm the occupant of the room. I can't think of anything else. Do you have any better ideas?'

'No,' replied Dolma. 'There's little else you can do, and it's not a bad idea. I've seen desk managers hand over keys to anybody who looks like a tourist. You might get away with it. But what if the man is still in his room and the keys are with him?'

'That shouldn't be a problem,' smiled Aditya. 'I'll pretend delight. You know, tell the manager, how wonderful! I thought I had missed him . . . or something like that.'

'Very clever, Aditya.'

'Yes, aren't I?' responded Aditya, ignoring Dolma's sarcasm. 'Will you wait for me in the lobby?'

'I shall. You go ahead, I'll follow later. Be careful, Aditya.' Dolma held out her hand.

Aditya held her hand and winked.

Dolma squeezed his fingers.

Aditya trooped across the sunlit yard, passing a colourful flower arrangement. Striding through large open doors, he entered the lobby. There were flowers there too. Several pots decorated the big, airy room. A man stood behind a wooden desk talking into a phone. He smiled at

Aditya as he walked to the desk. Cupping the mouth of the instrument, he asked, 'Can I help you, sir?'

'Keys to room number twenty-nine, please,' requested Aditya, smiling.

The man plucked a key from behind the desk, handing it to Aditya. Smiling cursorily, he returned his attention to the phone.

Aditya couldn't believe his luck. Clenching his fist around the key, he walked to a carpeted staircase. A sweeper in a blue uniform smiled at him on the first floor. Room twenty-nine was on the second floor. There was nobody on the dark landing. Unlocking the door, Aditya stepped in.

The room was comfortably sized and cosy. It was clear that the attendant had serviced the room. The bed was neatly made and the floor swept clean. A suitcase and a rucksack lay beside the bed in a corner. The furniture was simple and sparse: a cupboard, a desk and a chair.

Spotting an envelope on the desk, Aditya picked it up. 'Mr Akira' was the name scribbled in English on it. The envelope wasn't sealed, and Aditya slipped the contents out.

Airline tickets.

There were three. The first was in the name of Mr Akira. The ticket was to Chandigarh, and checking the date, Aditya saw that the flight was for the very same afternoon, at 3 p.m. The other tickets had Ladakhi names printed on them and were for the same flight.

Absorbing the information, Aditya glanced out of a window. Room twenty-nine was located directly above the hotel entrance, and he spotted Dolma below. The girl was walking to the entrance, her purse slung over her shoulder. He watched her enter the lobby before turning his gaze to the tickets in his hand.

The Japanese man was leaving today.

It made sense, thought Aditya. The man's work was done. Tsering had been captured. Could one of the other tickets be for Tsering? Was Mr Akira taking Tsering with him?

Aditya looked at his watch. It was past 10 a.m. He had less than two hours. Akira was his only lead to Tsering. There could be something in the room that might yield a clue. Aditya set about searching.

Dolma sat on a sofa in the lobby, leafing through a magazine. At the reception desk, the manager chatted on the phone. Sunlight warmed the room, streaming in through large windows. At one end was a door with a sign announcing 'Dining Hall'. Beside it, a flight of carpeted stairs led up. Men in blue uniforms flitted by, striding across the lobby.

Time passed, and the desk manager continued to talk on the phone.

Just then, a tall, gangly boy entered. He walked to the desk, and Dolma heard him ask for the keys to room number twenty-nine. Though the number sounded familiar, it failed to alert Dolma.

Ignoring the request, the desk manager continued to talk into the phone.

The boy waited meekly for a minute, then asked for the keys again.

138

This time, Dolma straightened. Aditya's room!

Dolma sprang to her feet. With quick strides, she crossed to the staircase. Walking briskly up the first flight, she broke into a run on the second. Locating room twenty-nine, she hissed Aditya's name.

Aditya jumped in fright, dropping the clothes hanger he was holding. Dolma! Why on earth had she so needlessly startled him?

'Aditya!' Dolma repeated in a low whisper. 'Somebody is coming to this room. I heard him ask for the keys. Come out fast . . . Oh no!' Dolma heard footsteps on the stairs. 'He is on his way up.'

Aditya lunged for the door. But the cupboard, the drawers . . . Everything was wide open. Working quickly, he pushed the drawers closed, shut the cupboard doors and smoothened the bedcover. As he strode to the door, he heard footsteps on the landing.

There was a soft knock on the door.

Aditya took a deep breath and opened the door.

A tall Ladakhi boy stood in the doorway, an uncertain expression on his face. The boy's gaze dropped when Aditya stared him in the eye. Head down, gazing at his shoes, he said something in Ladakhi.

Registering the boy's timidity, Aditya decided on offence, flying into a rage. 'Where is Akira?!' he exploded, glaring at the boy. 'Akira asked me to meet him here before 10 a.m. I've been waiting for more than half an hour, and there is no sign of him.'

'Akira is at Rinchen's place,' the boy answered meekly.

'Where is Rinchen's place?' demanded Aditya.

'Not far, sahib. Behind the mosque in the old city, below the palace. I can take you there.'

Aditya stared long and hard at the boy. He had to talk fast, not give the boy a chance to recover. 'It's not my business to go to Rinchen's place. You go tell Akira that I'm waiting for him here! I have only half an hour before I leave. All of us are upset about him messing up the kidnapping operation. Has he found the boy yet?'

'Yes, sahib, the boy is with Akira sahib at Rinchen's place. Akira sahib is flying the boy out of Leh in the afternoon. I have come here to collect the tickets.'

'Flying him out!' thundered Aditya. 'Who gave him permission? Is there a phone at Rinchen's place?'

'Yes, sahib . . . but I don't know the number.'

'You go to Akira quick! Tell him that I am waiting here for him and that he must come here immediately.'

'Yes, sahib,' mumbled the boy. 'Who should I tell him is waiting for him, sahib?'

'That is none of your business,' snapped Aditya. 'Take the tickets and go!'

The boy grabbed the tickets. Not daring to meet Aditya's eyes, he turned and fled from the room.

Aditya stood in the doorway breathing deeply. He jumped when the door opposite jerked open.

A pale-skinned man with red hair stuck his head out. 'Can we have some quiet here? Some of us are trying to sleep! Go downstairs if you want to argue.'

Aditya was in a combative mood, his adrenaline flowing. But realizing where he was, he controlled himself. He grinned weakly instead. 'Sorry,' he said apologetically.

The man snorted and banged his door shut.

Dolma appeared on the landing, stifling a giggle.

Aditya made a face at her. Stepping out of the room, he shut the door behind him. 'Let's go,' he said urgently. 'I don't want to lose the boy.'

They quickly ran down the stairs.

The desk manager had finally finished his call. They darted past him, out of the door into the sunshine.

'Forget the jeep,' said Aditya. 'Following him on foot will be easier.'

They ran across the yard to the gate. The road outside climbed steeply towards High Street. They spotted the boy marching along, halfway up the hill. A short distance ahead, he turned at a junction, disappearing behind a row of single-storeyed structures.

'He's taking the shortcut to the mosque,' panted Dolma, running beside Aditya.

There were shops on either side of the narrow road, and they had to push their way through tourists and traffic. Turning, they ran along an even narrower street that curved between short, dilapidated buildings.

Aditya saw no sign of the boy, but Dolma kept running and he followed. She led him between tiny houses that had been converted into cheap hotels. They finally spotted the boy near an intersection with a busy road. Their uphill dash had brought them closer to the boy.

He was barely fifty metres ahead now. They waited till the boy turned on to the road and then sprinted up the final section of the slope.

To Aditya's surprise, he discovered that they had reached High Street. The mosque lay directly ahead. The boy had crossed the road and was walking to the mosque. The street bustled with activity. Drawing confidence from the cover of the crowd, Dolma and Aditya drew closer to the boy. The boy turned right a few shops short of the mosque, entering a narrow gully, and then swung left at the next intersection.

Leading them to the head of the lane, the boy passed through a big gate with solid, imposing doors. Aditya knew where he was. Dolma had brought him here before. They had entered the old city. The area was quiet. The winding lanes here and the antiquated stone buildings had escaped change, remaining undisturbed for centuries.

The crowds fell behind. The tiny gullies of the old city were deserted. Aditya and Dolma were forced to fall back. The boy led them up a steep gully, ascending the hill behind High Street. A set of rock-hewn steps appeared. The boy mounted them, climbing to a large wooden door, which he pushed open and disappeared behind.

Aditya found it difficult to define the structure the boy had entered. It had been built in an era before the modern building evolved. Above the door were windows cut out of sand-brick walls. It was a tall house with an indeterminate number of levels. The gully on which the house stood continued beyond, disappearing round the corner ahead.

Aditya urged Dolma forward. 'Come on. Don't stop. Walk past the house.'

Passing the building could be risky. Anyone looking down from the windows would spot them. Dolma started to protest, but Aditya grabbed her hand and walked determinedly forward.

Nobody shouted.

Pigeons fluttered as they crossed the danger zone and rounded the bend ahead. Aditya kept walking, climbing along the steeply rising lane till it ended abruptly against the wall of a large, stone cliff.

Rock-hewn steps, carved out of the cliff face, led upward. Ascending them, Dolma and Aditya emerged from the shadows into bright sunshine. A panoramic view lay spread below them. The mosque and High Street were directly below. The polo ground was visible in the distance, and the old palace towered above to their left.

Dolma caught Aditya's arm, pointing. 'That's the house the boy entered.'

Immediately below were the roofs of the old houses they had walked past, each festooned with fluttering prayer flags. Satellite dishes bristled from most of the terraces. The roof Dolma had pointed out had a black water tank. Several potted plants were scattered on its flat surface.

Aditya examined the row of roofs. They were all packed together, close enough for jumping from terrace to terrace, if one were so inclined. A plan formed in Aditya's head. He could do it. Getting to the terrace that Dolma had indicated would not be difficult.

Suddenly, Dolma whispered urgently.

Aditya saw her crouch behind a pile of rocks. Aditya bent down too. Three men had emerged from the house. Hurrying down the steps, they ran down the lane, back along the way Aditya and Dolma had come.

Aditya's eyes met Dolma's.

Each knew what the other was thinking. The Japanese man was in the house. They were certain now. The boy must have talked to him. The story Aditya had spun must have stirred things up. The men had been despatched as a result, sent to find Aditya. There was no reason to doubt any more. Not only was the Japanese man in the house, but Tsering was also there.

Dolma sneaked back to Aditya, crawling all the way.

Aditya cleared his throat. 'We are going to have to split up, Dolma.'

Dolma looked up questioningly.

'The two of us sitting here together doesn't make sense. If somebody discovers us, we'll both be caught. Those steps ahead lead back to the city. Go down to High Street and wait for me at the post office there.'

'I see,' said Dolma, a hint of rebellion in her voice. 'And what are you going to do while I wait?'

'I don't know what the Japanese man will do next, Dolma. Things have gone very wrong for him. He could—'

'You intend to try and rescue Tsering,' interrupted Dolma. 'I saw you staring at the roofs, Aditya. I can see the way your mind works.' Dolma flashed an unexpected smile. 'We think alike, Aditya. This is a good time to sneak up on the Japanese man—when he's least expecting it. It's worth a try. But why you? Why not me?'

Aditya had no answer. 'There could be trouble—' he stuttered.

The Ladakhi girl cut him off once more. 'The male in you is going to say that you are stronger and that you can handle trouble better, right?' Without waiting for an answer, she continued. 'You are right. Yes, you are stronger, but you have certain impressions about women that need straightening. I promise to work on you sometime, but not now. I will go now. I'll be waiting for you next to the post office. If you don't return in half an hour, I'll get help. Is that okay?'

Aditya nodded.

Dolma smiled. She placed her arms around Aditya and hugged him. 'Be careful,' she whispered. 'Don't do anything stupid. Promise?'

'Promise,' replied Aditya.

Reaching up, she kissed him on his cheek. Then waving goodbye, she turned away.

ROOFTOP AVENUE

Aditya touched his cheek. Dolma had kissed him.

'Wow!' he whispered as he watched her walk along the cliff edge. The kiss was an entirely unexpected gesture. He wondered whether she would regret her moment of softness when they met next.

Dolma soon disappeared behind a cliff wall, and Aditya shifted his gaze back to the roofs. He walked forward along the ledge till he found a spot where its rocky edge approached within a few feet of the roof immediately below him.

Aditya jumped.

Landing comfortably on the roof, he crossed its stone surface and jumped on to the next one. The roofs were all at the same level and separated by just three to four feet. In little more than a minute, Aditya was crouching on the roof beside the one he intended to enter.

Aditya waited.

Sounds of the city wafted up from below. The sun shone brightly, and across the valley, the Stok mountains were still blanketed by the clouds. Gazing at the mountains, Aditya recollected that he was to leave for them soon. He looked at his watch. It was 11.10 a.m. But time no longer bothered him. Raghu's expedition wasn't important any more. Tsering was here . . . He had to be rescued.

The black plastic tank loomed large on the terrace ahead. Sunflowers and daisies blossomed in neatly laid pots beside it. On the mosaic-tiled floor of the terrace, Aditya spotted a dark rectangular opening. The terrace was empty except for a flock of pigeons shuffling beside the tank.

The pigeons scattered when Aditya jumped. He landed softly near the flowerpots and crept to the shadowed opening. Stone steps led down, terminating at a door. Though the door was open, the passageway beyond lay in shadow. The sound of a television set was faintly audible.

Aditya descended the steps, his sneakers making no sound at all. There was a strong smell of food, and he heard the sizzle of a frying pan. On reaching the open door, Aditya crouched and halted.

The passageway was long. Like a tunnel, it disappeared into the gloom ahead. Pools of light from open doors illuminated it in sections. Opposite Aditya was a half-open kitchen door. Inside, he saw a man stirring a pan. Several pots steamed beside the pan, and freshly cut vegetables were heaped on the counter nearby.

If the cook glanced over his shoulder, he would spot Aditya. Aditya had no intention of waiting for that to happen. With his eyes on the cook, he slipped into the passage.

This house had been cut from the mountainside. Aditya could tell because the floor was original cliff stone, smoothened over the years. Aditya felt uncomfortable. Turning his back on the open kitchen door worried him. The cook could step out any time. But there was nothing Aditya could do about it. The risk was necessary if he was to rescue Tsering.

Aditya soon came to the next open door. He crouched, bending till his head was a foot above the ground. He then slowly edged his head forward, towards the opening. But as he did so, he heard the sound of muffled footsteps. Backing away swiftly, he pressed himself against the wall. Swallowing, he waited for the feet to emerge. Seconds ticked away, but nobody stepped out. The footsteps continued. There was a rhythm to them, a number of steps receding, followed by an equal number approaching. The cycle repeated itself over and over again.

A full minute passed before Aditya mustered the courage to lower himself again. At floor height, he popped his head around the door frame and peeped inside. A man was walking down the length of a long room. His hands were clasped behind his back, his head angled to the ground. The floor the man walked upon was carpeted. Sunlight entered from two slit-like windows, and Aditya spied a table, sofas and chairs before withdrawing his head. Tsering was not in the room. Nor was there anyone else besides the pacing man.

Aditya waited till the man strode down the length of the room before slipping past the door. He tiptoed quickly to the next open door. The noise of the television was louder now. He flattened himself along the cold floor and, once again, edged his face forward to peer through the open door.

There were two men in the room. They sat on the floor, facing a television set. Curtains had been pulled across the window slits. A popular Hindi movie song blared from the set, and the men were absorbed in the gyrations of the heroine on the screen. Aditya slid past the door. In the gloom, he spotted another open doorway.

As he stole forward, a shrill sound reverberated across the hall.

Convinced he had set off an alarm, Aditya leapt rabbit-like into the doorway ahead. His heart thudded wildly as he pressed himself into the darkest corner of the room.

The sound ended as abruptly as it had begun.

Aditya heard somebody shouting in a language he did not understand. There was anger and alarm in the voice. It dawned on Aditya that the angry voice was shouting into a phone and that it was the ringing of the instrument that had so terribly frightened him.

The receiver was slammed down with great strength and the voice shouted again.

There was movement within the television room. Feet thudded out of the door into the passageway. Aditya became tensed for a moment, but he relaxed when he heard the footsteps running to the opposite end of the passageway. The angry voice had summoned the television viewers. Although there were more rooms to search,

Aditya decided to stay put. The burst of activity had made movement hazardous.

It wasn't long before Aditya heard the sound of feet striding down the passageway again—this time in his direction. Huddling against the wall, he saw two shadows pass by. The footsteps stopped a short distance ahead. There was the sound of a latch being pulled back. Harsh words were spoken. Then the shadows returned, but now Aditya saw three—two tall and between them a short one, barely half the size of the other two.

Tsering!

Aditya felt a surge of exhilaration. He had found Tsering! But the rush of victory was fleeting. How was he going to rescue Tsering from the clutches of his captors?

Aditya closed his eyes, forcing himself to think. He puzzled over the reason for the sudden activity. Things had been quiet when he had entered, but the phone call had changed all that. Men had been summoned, and Tsering had been fetched. Had Tsering's captors been waiting for this call? Was Tsering being taken away? If that was the case, then Aditya did not have much time. Hiding in the dark room was not going to get him anywhere. He would have to do something.

Aditya poked his head out of the doorway. There was no one in the passageway. Someone was speaking loudly in the carpeted room. Crockery clattered in the kitchen. Aditya stepped into the passageway. Tiptoeing past the empty television room, he halted and crouched at the doorway of the carpeted room.

Aditya was worried about the cook. The man could blow his cover if he decided to step into the passageway. But there was little he could do about it. He would have to live with the possibility. Aditya turned his attention to the carpeted room, staring at its door. The door was thick, solid and pushed back against the wall of the room. It had a brass latch and a handle that was level with his head.

Lowering himself to the cold stone floor, he edged his head forward so he could peep through the open doorway. The room inside was long and rectangular. Halfway down was the man doing the talking, partly hidden by the men who had been watching television earlier. They stood with their backs to Aditya, one holding Tsering firmly. The man who was talking was striding back and forth across the room. Now Aditya could see his face. In spite of the dim light, there was no mistaking his East Asian features—Aditya had finally found the Japanese man.

Aditya withdrew his head. Rescuing Tsering wasn't going to be easy. There were three grown men in the room, and additionally there was a cook who, like a wild card, could appear at any moment. Aditya looked at the kitchen door. The clinking of crockery reassured him. He was safe . . . for the time being at least.

Aditya leaned against the wall. His chest felt constricted. His lungs were heaving at an abnormal pace, as if he had just completed a cross-country race. Fear! Aditya could feel its icy tentacles creeping into the very core of his being. His hands shook, and the passageway reeled before his eyes.

This was not the time to sink into despair. He had to think positively. There was no question of retreating—time had run out. His intrusion into the Japanese man's hotel room had unsettled the kidnapper. The shouting and the pacing indicated so. The man was rattled. He was bound to act now. Tsering being pulled out of his cage confirmed that something was going to happen. The man could be planning to smuggle him away to another location or to fly him straight out of the city.

Aditya lowered his head and peeped into the room again.

Tsering was standing unattended. But like a wall, the guards stood between him and Aditya. The Japanese man paced and continued to talk.

The phone rang once more. The men's attention was drawn to the instrument. Aditya seized the opportunity. Crouching, he entered the room. He crawled rapidly forward, halting behind a sofa.

The Japanese man strode to the phone and picked it up.

The man's back was turned towards Aditya. Tsering's guards stood barely three strides from where Aditya crouched. This was the moment. Aditya had to strike while their attention was focused on the instrument. But he hesitated. He needed to distract them further. If he could startle them, throw them off balance, those additional moments could make the difference. Aditya's eyes darted across the room. Amidst the sofas and chairs was a table and on it was a glass jug half-filled with water.

Aditya rose. He was now in full view of anyone turning around. With quick, sure-footed strides, he reached the table and lifted the jug. The carpet deadened the sound of his movements. The Japanese man stood at the far wall, speaking heatedly into the phone. In between stood Tsering and the two guards. Aditya chose a spot to the right of the guards, and like a grenade, he lobbed the jug forward.

The jug crashed, smashing into pieces. Its effect was electrifying. Tsering's guards jumped, and the Japanese man dropped the receiver in fright.

Aditya charged forward.

With great momentum, he slammed into Tsering's guards. The crash of the jug had already unsettled the men, and the following scything impact swept them off their feet.

'Tsering!' hissed Aditya. 'Come on!'

He reached forward and grabbed the startled boy, swinging him round and pushing him to the door.

The Japanese man stared in shock.

Aditya paid no attention to him. From the corner of his eye, he could see the two men recovering. Tsering had fallen to the ground. Aditya grabbed a wooden chair and flung it at the guard who first rose from the ground.

Tsering was still finding his feet. Aditya ran to the boy. Half carrying him, he propelled the little Tibetan out of the door, into the passageway.

The Japanese man was screaming.

The guards were on their feet and running towards Aditya.

Halting at the door, Aditya grabbed its latch and yanked. Rusty hinges protested loudly as the door swung towards him. Aditya heaved with all his strength.

Shouting, the men lunged, reaching forward. Barely an inch separated their outstretched fingers and the wheeling door, but that was enough. The door slammed into place and Aditya bolted the latch.

Tsering lay sprawled in the passageway, his face shining with the most joyful smile Aditya had ever seen.

'Get up!' shouted Aditya, leaping over him.

A man wearing an apron emerged from the kitchen.

Aditya did not break step. He accelerated instead, charging forward.

The cook hurriedly attempted to step back.

Aditya's shoulder caught him in mid-stride, launching him off his feet. Hurled backwards, the hapless man fell with a crash.

Aditya glanced back at Tsering. The boy was on his feet and running behind him.

The latched door of the carpeted room shook.

Aditya sprinted up the stairs, blinking as he emerged into harsh sunshine on the terrace. He waited for Tsering, and when the boy emerged, he grabbed him, leading him to the edge of the roof. Tsering leapt without hesitation. Aditya glanced behind before following Tsering. No one had emerged as yet. The cook was probably still regaining his feet. He had yet to open the latched door. A few precious moments were still available. Aditya jumped. Landing comfortably on the next roof, he kept running to its far edge.

'Oh no!' he exclaimed. The roof ahead was too distant for Tsering. The jump was impossible for the boy. Aditya wheeled. He spotted steps leading down into the house.

Tsering had already chosen the option and was running down the steps. Aditya followed.

The house was built identically to the one that had held Tsering. There was a similar passageway connecting the rooms. A lady's voice shouted indignantly as Aditya sprinted past the kitchen. Two children stuck their faces out of the door of a room from which a television blared.

'Namaste,' smiled Aditya as he followed Tsering. He had to leap sideways to avoid an old man standing at the far end of the passageway, gazing on in astonishment.

Tsering was running down a flight of stairs.

The steps were uneven, and it was dark. After stumbling once, Aditya slowed, feeling his way forward. Keeping up with Tsering was impossible. The boy was far more sure-footed than him.

Sunlight shone from a door that Tsering had opened. Aditya emerged into a narrow lane. His heart jumped. He knew exactly where he was. The gully he had followed to get here lay to his right. But . . . Aditya stamped his foot in frustration. Tsering had turned the other way, and it was too late to stop him.

Aditya followed Tsering as he ripped down the path. He looked skywards when a shadow flitted overhead. Aditya gritted his teeth. It was one of the kidnappers, leaping between the roofs above. Aditya bowed his head and sprinted after Tsering.

Suddenly, there were no more buildings. The path petered out at the bottom of a dusty slope. Aditya looked back. There were four men on the roofs. The Japanese man was the closest. As he watched, the man vaulted to a lower roof. His next jump would bring him to ground level. Tsering had halted on the slope and had turned to look at Aditya. Behind Tsering, Aditya saw the walls of the old palace.

'There!' shouted Aditya, pointing at the palace.

Tsering didn't understand English, but Aditya's pointing finger clearly indicated the direction he had in mind.

They pounded up the slope. Aditya, who was far stronger, soon overtook Tsering. Several trails meandered across the dusty slope, crossing one another. Aditya stumbled over loosely packed earth. His throat was dry, and he panted heavily as his lungs battled for oxygen in the sparse mountain air. Tsering fell steadily behind Aditya. On the last section, as he neared the palace, the incline turned steeper. Aditya halted, looking back. Their pursuers were strung out along the slope. The closest was the Japanese man, barely ten metres behind Tsering.

'Come on, Tsering,' urged Aditya.

Somehow, against all odds, the little boy managed a smile. As he approached Aditya, he raised his palm, requesting Aditya for a high five.

'Go, Tsering!' yelled Aditya, smacking the proffered hand.

The tiny lama scampered past.

The Japanese man was close enough for Aditya to hear his breathing. Turning, Aditya followed the now visibly tired boy. Sweat poured down Aditya's eyelids, blurring his vision. He pushed Tsering from behind, helping him.

The Japanese man's shadow darkened the earth at Aditya's feet.

The slope ended just metres ahead. Aditya accelerated. Passing Tsering, he grabbed his hand, pulling him over the final stretch.

PALACE DRAMA

The palace grounds had been levelled into a flat courtyard. In the middle of the courtyard was a huge pandal with a raised platform opposite it. Plastic chairs were arranged in rows under the pandal's shade and a crowd was seated there. Cultural shows were organized regularly for tourists at the palace, and a live show was in progress.

Still holding Tsering's hand, Aditya ran towards the pandal. The Japanese man stumbled into the courtyard, following them.

The spectators took no heed of the drama behind them, their attention fixed on the stage. The boys sprinted towards the crowd with the Japanese man in hot pursuit.

There were several rows of seats facing the stage. The show wasn't houseful, and Aditya spotted empty chairs. The boys pounded into the covered area under the pandal. Choosing a row halfway down, Aditya entered it, barging forward. Irate glances were cast their way as they stamped and stumbled forward. Finding a pair of empty seats, the boys settled themselves.

Ignoring the resentful spectators seated about him, Aditya turned his head. The Japanese man stood at the end of their row, breathing heavily, staring at them. For the first time, Aditya had a clear view of his features. Though the man wasn't tall, he was powerfully built. His skin was pale, and his hair was long and untidy. His lower lip was curled back in what seemed like a permanent sneer. If looks could kill, Aditya would have been dead. The expression on the man's face was murderous.

Aditya turned his gaze, looking further back. The guards and the cook had arrived. They stood at the last row. Two more men were climbing into the courtyard. Aditya's heart sank when one of the guards turned and motioned the men forward. Reinforcements had arrived.

The men quickly arranged themselves around the gathering. Two replaced the Japanese man at the head of their row and another pair positioned themselves on the far side of their row. A fifth man guarded the rear of the pandal. The Japanese man stood in the front, near the stage.

A lively performance was being enacted on the stage. A ferocious looking yak danced to a slow beat accompanied by music blaring through a pair of loudspeakers. The yak obviously wasn't real—it was men dancing, draped in a fine costume. Tsering suddenly broke into laughter and so did the audience when the yak, adopting a comical posture, kicked out its rear legs.

Aditya was too tense to pay attention to the antics on stage. In spite of the presence of the crowd, he did not feel safe. The Japanese man was not going to give up. He had

159

drawn a noose around them. There was bound to be trouble after the show. The crowd comprised mostly of tourists, and Aditya knew he couldn't expect much help from them.

Beyond the stage, the ground sloped upwards and a road led to the palace. An army vehicle was parked on the road. Aditya's spirits lifted. Army officers could be useful. They might protect them. Aditya scanned the audience, searching for officers. He saw a special row of seats to one side of the stage. Two women were sitting alone on elaborate throne-like seats. One of them had turned and was staring in his direction. When Aditya looked at her, she waved. The lady was Reena's mother.

Aditya's heart leapt at the sight of Mrs Bhonagiri. She continued to wave, pointing at empty seats beside her. Turning, Mrs Bhonagiri raised her arm to summon someone. An army jawan with a machine gun slung across his shoulder was standing beside a stone wall. Responding to Mrs Bhonagiri's call, he strode smartly forward and bent respectfully at her side. The soldier listened carefully, then marched down the row of seats and halted beside the boys' row.

Aditya needed no second invitation. With a grin the size of a spaceship, he requested Tsering to follow. The jawan waited sentry-like for the boys and then escorted them to where the ladies were seated. Neither the Japanese man nor his men interfered, wisely refraining from tangling with the armed soldier.

Mrs Bhonagiri, unlike her shy and reserved daughter, was a bubbly, effervescent lady. She welcomed Aditya with a large smile. 'How nice to see you, Aditya. Meet my dear friend, Polly. This is Polly's first visit to Leh, and I brought her here to see the palace. But what are you doing here, Aditya? Reena told me that you and Vikram were leaving on a trek today.'

The trek! Aditya had completely forgotten. Maybe he could still make it. Aditya looked at his watch. Barely five minutes remained before 12 p.m. sharp.

'What's the matter, Aditya?' inquired Mrs Bhonagiri. 'Something wrong? You look like you've seen a ghost.' Mrs Bhonagiri's tone switched to a motherly one. 'Do you know that you look an absolute mess? I shall tell your mother, Aditya. Last year when she was here, you were always well turned out. Look at you now: shabbily dressed; mud on your face and clothes. The things you boys get up to when your parents are away!' Mrs Bhonagiri shook her head reprovingly.

'Auntie!' said Aditya urgently. 'Thank god you reminded me! I didn't realize how late it is. Can your driver drop me to the city? Please! My group will be leaving shortly. I'll return the car immediately.'

'Yes dear, of course you can borrow my car. But my word, you boys are amazing!' Mrs Bhonagiri gazed in wonderment at Aditya. 'Don't you ever plan your day? My husband always wanted a boy. I'm thankful we have a girl instead. Girls are clean and hygienic, and they at least have some idea of time!'

Mrs Bhonagiri signalled once more to the soldier. When he arrived, she issued instructions to him.

'Go with him,' said Mrs Bhonagiri. 'He will escort you to the car, and the driver will drop you. Bye, Aditya. Have a good time. When do we see you next?'

'In two weeks, auntie, that's when we will be back. Thank you so much. Say bye to Reena from me . . . and auntie, one more thing. Will you please send Dolma a message that my friend Tsering and I have left together on the trek with Raghu?'

Mrs Bhonagiri assured Aditya that Dolma would get the message.

The show was still going on. The yak had been replaced by a dance troupe. The audience was enjoying itself. Tourists were dancing in the aisles, imitating the group on stage.

Aditya stood up. 'Thanks, auntie,' he said, his words heartfelt.

Mrs Bhonagiri flashed a bright smile. 'Any time. Hurry now. Have a great time.'

Aditya smiled at Mrs Bhonagiri and her friend. Then holding Tsering's hand, he walked towards the army jeep.

The Japanese man started forward. He and two of his men walked on Aditya's right. The remaining men kept pace with Aditya to his left. Two more kidnappers cut directly towards them, attempting to block their path. Tsering shrank towards Aditya. But Aditya was unperturbed. Raising a hand, he called out to the army jawan. The jawan, noticing the threatening stance of the kidnappers, strode towards Aditya, unhitching his weapon.

The Japanese man spoke sharply, restraining his men. Aditya looked at him. The man's face was surprisingly composed. The thunderous rage that Aditya had seen earlier had been replaced by a calm, collected expression. His eyes met Aditya's.

Aditya caught himself. He was all set to grin and gloat at the man, but the look directed at him changed his mind. Aditya had never dreamt that eyes could convey such hostility. The look chilled him to the bone. A shiver ran through him. Aditya knew then that he was up against a man with great resolve. He might have won the battle for the moment, but his opponent was not going to give up. The war for Tsering would go on.

'*Chale*, sahib?' asked the jawan.

Still holding Tsering's hand, Aditya walked to the jeep, his eyes locked with the Japanese man's. It was the man who finally broke the spell. Looking away, he barked something at his men.

Aditya halted beside the jeep. The jeep driver, dressed smartly in fatigues, held the door open. When they were seated, the jawan closed the door and saluted.

Aditya returned the salute and smiled.

Tsering already had a big grin on his face. But Aditya was still tense. His eyes darted about the road, searching for other vehicles. He was thankful to see that there were none.

Aditya's spirits perked up when the driver started the jeep. At no point during the drama had it seemed that they might make a clean getaway. Now it appeared that they would. Someone was pulling at his shirt. Aditya turned.

Tsering was looking up at him. His hand was held out, his palm facing Aditya.

Aditya grinned at the boy and held his hand above his head.

Their palms met in a high five.

Through the window, Aditya saw that the Japanese man wasn't sitting by idly. He and his men were running down the mountain slope to the city.

Aditya glanced at his watch. Less than a minute remained for 12 p.m. sharp. The Khardung La junction wasn't far, but it would be touch-and-go.

As the jeep drove along, Aditya wondered what to do with Tsering. Should he hand him over to Meme Chacko? But Aditya wasn't sure that Meme Chacko could keep Tsering safe. For that matter, was Tsering safe anywhere in Leh? The grim determination Aditya had seen on the Japanese man's face convinced him that Tsering wasn't.

Aditya made up his mind. He would take Tsering along on the snow leopard expedition. Tsering could be whisked out of the city without anyone being the wiser. The Japanese man would be at a loss. Smuggling Tsering out would stump him. By the time he realized Tsering wasn't in Leh, they would be gone. No one knew where Vikram and he were going. No one except a handful of friends. Friends who would never breathe a word to the Japanese man. Importantly, the area they were headed for was a remote corner of Ladakh, far from cities and roads. Tsering would be safe there.

Aditya looked once more at his watch.

It was almost noon. The palace had fallen behind, and the city lay below them. Aditya had not yet told the driver where he was to be dropped.

'Khardung La junction,' said Aditya.

The driver nodded.

The Khardung La junction was still some distance ahead. They wouldn't get there by 12 p.m. Would Raghu hold the jeeps for him? Though Aditya prayed he would, he knew Raghu wouldn't.

The jeep reached the outskirts of the city at noon. There were pedestrians on the road now, and the driver honked to overtake a truck. Aditya bit his lip in frustration as the driver refused to let them pass.

'*Jaldi!*' he urged the army driver.

The driver honked loudly, and the truck reluctantly gave way.

The junction was a busy area. Aditya scanned the road for Raghu's jeeps. He saw several buses. There were jeeps there too, parked amidst scooters and private cars. Aditya looked hard at each of them. It was a minute past 12 p.m. when the driver halted at the junction.

Beside a giant prayer wheel on the side of the road was a jeep that was driving away. Aditya jumped on to the road.

'VIKRAM!' he shouted, unmindful of the traffic.

There was a screech of brakes as the truck they had just overtaken ground to a halt behind him—Aditya had jumped directly into its path.

Vikram was at his wits' end. Where was Aditya? He could not imagine embarking on the expedition alone, without his friend. Yet that was what was about to happen.

Everyone had assembled at the junction by 11.30 a.m. Vikram had met the other members of the expedition and had chatted with them. Time had passed, and Vikram had turned increasingly nervous.

Raghu had been uncompromising. Two jeeps carrying some of the participants had left a few minutes before noon. He then gave Vikram a piece of his mind, ranting about Aditya and how careless the younger generation had become. Raghu instructed everybody to be seated in the remaining jeep at 12 p.m. Vikram stood outside, trying to delay as long as he could, but Raghu would have none of it. He shouted at Vikram, ordering him to board the jeep. With a heavy heart, Vikram settled himself in the vehicle. The driver started the engine.

Vikram did not see Aditya because he was looking down the road from the city, not the one from Khardung La. But the jarring squeal of brakes and the angry honking of a truck turned Vikram's head.

'ADITYA!' shouted Vikram. 'It's him. There he is!'

Vikram was seated next to a pretty American girl, and she backed off in alarm when he erupted in delight.

Raghu instructed the driver to halt.

Aditya was tearing down the road, and there was a little boy running behind him. Could it be . . . Yes, it was!

'TSERING!' Vikram shouted.

The occupants of the jeep looked strangely at Vikram, but he didn't care. His joy knew no bounds. Tsering! Aditya had found Tsering! Vikram whooped with delight.

A young lady with dark hair opened the rear door of the jeep. Aditya was running with his hands held above his head, a triumphant expression on his face. Vikram held his hand out and Aditya smacked it as he jumped into the jeep.

Vikram turned, looking at little Tsering. His eyes were on fire and his face had an expression of the purest joy Vikram had ever seen. The little Tibetan leapt into Vikram's arms.

The lady pulled the door shut and the jeep rolled forward.

Unmindful of the others, the three friends clung to one another. Tears flowed down Vikram's cheeks. Aditya's eyes were moist too. Tsering, the young lama, smiled happily between them. His face was radiant, and his eyes glowed with contentment.

Aditya did not bother to keep a lookout for the Japanese man. He was certain they had escaped undetected. The man had been outwitted. Tsering was now beyond his reach. Yes, Tsering was safe! He could say that with absolute certainty.

At last, Aditya could think of the wonderful trip that lay ahead of them. Through the windows, he caught a glimpse of the mountains to which they were headed. The mists had parted, and jagged snow-capped peaks were visible. They would soon be amidst the peaks, walking their rugged trails. The grey ghost of the Himalayas lived up there. They were about to enter the home of the snow leopard. Aditya could feel the thrill creeping through his veins. Yes, with Tsering beside them, Vikram and he would find the animal.

READ MORE IN THE SERIES

Ranthambore Adventure

THIS IS THE STORY OF A TIGER

Once a helpless ball of fur, Genghis emerges as a mighty predator, the king of the forest. But the jungle isn't just his kingdom. Soon, Genghis finds himself fighting for his skin against equally powerful predators but of a different kind—humans.

The very same ones that Vikram and Aditya get embroiled with when they attempt to lay their hands on a diary that belongs to a ruthless tiger poacher. Worlds collide when an ill-fated encounter plunges the boys and their friend Aarti into a thrilling chase that takes them deep into the magnificent game park of Ranthambore.

Journey through the wilderness, brimming with tiger lore, with a tale set in one of India's most splendid destinations.